Liz Lovelock

THE

RIGHT

Guy

MY GUY #4

Cover Design by Ben Ellis from Be Designs
Photographer: Reggie Deanching from The Stable & Models of RplusMphoto
Models: Vince Alexander Azzopardi
Edited by Lauren from Creating Ink
Proofread by Jen Lockwood Editing
Formatted by Tami at Integrity Formatting

www.lizlovelockauthor.com

THE
RIGHT
Guy
MY GUY #4

CHAPTER
One

Charity

I can't believe I'm back here again.

Stepping into my old bedroom feels like time has warped, like it's playing some kind of sick joke on me. The smell of musty old things immediately hits my senses. That mold—mixed with some other scent I would rather forget—leeches into me, making me screw up my nose at the disgusting odor that lingers all around me.

White curtains with a lace trim line the windows; only now the trim has browned with age. I quickly walk over, moving them out of the way, and shove the window sash up to let in some fresh air.

As I swing around, I notice the walls are still painted pale pink—well, sort of. The pink has turned into more of an off-pink now, and some of the paint is peeling from the ceiling. Even my original pink bedding from when I was here last is perfectly made on the bed.

That's going to be the first thing I change.

Why did she not update the decor?

My bags drop from my shoulder and fall to the floor with a heavy thud.

Attempting to find something—anything—that will help me connect with this room and my past, I expel a heavy sigh and close my eyes tightly. Panic stabs right through me as anxiety takes hold, while a memory of the way my father's loud, angry voice used to echo through these familiar, yet not-so-familiar, walls.

I release my breath and open my eyes, endeavoring to push thoughts of that man far from my mind.

I didn't have to come here. I could've stayed exactly where I was—in a house that now belongs to me, considering my father has passed away. Only, I want nothing to do with that house anymore. That's why I came here. I need closure because, for years, I waited for my mother to come to me. When she didn't, it left me feeling inadequate. Lacking. Wanting more from a mother who simply wasn't able to provide the motherly love when I needed it the most. And quite frankly, she never fought for me.

They say when parents split, it's the kids who suffer. Well, I most certainly did. I never got to know my mother. My father, a decent man—or so I thought—left with me in tow when I was nine and told me my mother was unfit to take care of me. Now he's gone, and I'm here with her, ten years later, in her home.

This is not exactly how I remember it, and she has a new family now.

A family I didn't know existed.

My father lied to me.

Everything he ever told me about my mom was fabricated. He said she was unfit to care for a child and had not one ounce of motherly love in her body.

When he first took me away, I remember begging him to take me back. I missed my mom. I missed her touch. I remember living in this house, and I know these walls hold the answers to my past and where my life all went wrong.

I waited for the day when Mom would show up at my dad's door to take me back home.

Only, she never came.

I wish I knew all the details of what came to pass, but my father died with his lies, and now I hope my mom can help me discover the truth.

"Are you all settled in?" My mother hovers by the doorway, which makes this whole situation even more uncomfortable than it already is.

Shrugging, I say, "Uh… yeah. Perhaps I need to redecorate." I smile.

She laughs, a hint of nervousness coming through in the tone. "Oh, yes, of course. I didn't want to go ahead with changing anything unless you had a say."

I swallow then reply, "Thanks."

I stare at her as she twists her fingers nervously, an action I am mirroring. My hands freeze and then drop to my sides. The more I look at her, the more I see myself. And the more I see, the more I want to know her. I have a million questions, but not today. Everything is still so raw, like a graze on my knee that stings every time it's touched. Only, this graze is on my heart.

Her shining green eyes are masking a shimmer of tears. "Charity, I *am* sorry about your father. I'm so sorry for failing you. I should have done better." Her voice cracks, and the lump in my throat returns. It seems to be a permanent fixture lately whenever someone brings *him* up. That familiar pain, the agony that stabs me through the heart.

"Mom…" I sigh, unable to form the right words, finally all I can manage is. "Thanks," I don't know this woman. I have no idea whether she knows the pain I have been through.

"Anyway, if there's anything you need, please let me know. Also, I'm not sure what food you like. If you can leave me a list of things you might want, I'll be sure to get them for you from the grocery store." She steps forward. I'm sure she's going in for a hug, but then the mask pulls over her eyes, and she quickly shifts back and exits my room, shutting the door with a quiet click on her way out.

A sigh escapes my tight lungs as I collapse onto the double bed covered in a pink blanket. My body feels as though it's run a marathon, yet I've only been in the car. It was a very stale, silent drive with Mom. She tried to make small talk, but I didn't feel like speaking. Forming a relationship with someone I hardly know is going to take time—and lots of it.

Leaving behind what few friends I had was difficult. People here, in this house and town, are lost memories for me.

There is this one face that's stuck with me over the years, though. His blue eyes were in my dreams for a long time after I left. Jase… my *old* best friend.

Three very light knocks at my door drag me from my thoughts. "Come in," I call. The handle clicks and slowly opens.

Leaning over, I try and see who's there.

Is it Mom?

A young girl pokes her head around, and I sit, welcoming her with a smile.

"Who are you?" she asks without hesitation.

"I'm Charity. Who are you?" I shuffle on my bed and tap it for her to come and sit with me.

In skips a gorgeous little girl, like she doesn't have a care in the world. "I'm Grace. Momma told me you're my big sister. I've always wanted to meet you." She climbs onto my mattress and sits with her legs crossed. Familiar, bright-green eyes like mine, like Mom's, stare back at me. *Sister.* Mom told me about her, but seeing her now is surreal. She's tall, probably comes up to just under my arms, and is wearing the cutest little pink frilly dress with a bow placed perfectly in her hair.

I suck my bottom lip between my teeth and bite. I've never had a sibling. A small amount of anger bubbles inside me toward my dad. Why did he keep so much from me?

"I am your sister. How old are you?"

Grace wriggles up, sitting tall as though she's in a classroom. "I'm seven this year," she says proudly. Her hair is long and dark, like mine, and those questioning eyes burrow a place right into my heart.

"Wow, that's a good age. How are you liking school?" Oh my goodness, I want to know so much about my sister. I've already missed seven years of her life; I don't want to miss a second more.

Dad never met anyone new—well, no one I knew about. Mostly, I spent my time on my own. Dad never allowed me to have friends over, so I learned quickly that books were my best friends. Every chance I got, I had a new title in hand; of course, they all had to have a happily ever after, simply so I could get the feeling of love. Even if it was just from between the pages of books. Love was something Dad sadly couldn't give me, so I sought it elsewhere.

She rolls her eyes, and I laugh. "School is okay. I like seeing my friends. I don't like my teacher, though. She yells a lot, and it's scary when she does." She pauses a moment. Her head drops and then bounces back up. "I'm glad you're here. Mom has always told me I had an older sister that she hoped I would meet one day."

An overwhelming warmth spreads through my chest. Here I'd thought she'd completely forgotten about me. I was wrong.

"Thank you," I choke out. "I'm glad I get to meet you as well. I hope we can become good friends."

Grace slips off my bed and comes to stand in front of me. She doesn't hold back; instead, she throws her arms around my neck and squeezes. My eyes well up, and a quick tear escapes. She smells like strawberries with a hint of apple. I hold on to her tiny frame and wish for these moments to never stop.

"Ah you're kind of squishing me." Her voice sounds strained. My arms instantly loosen.

"Sorry."

Grace grins. "That's okay. You give good hugs."

I laugh. "So do you." It's as though the crater of emptiness I've been experiencing most of my life has suddenly filled up the moment her arms went around my neck.

She leans back and dances on her toes, clapping her hands. "I can't wait to show you my room, and I want you to see my favorite park down the road."

"Hey, I might be able to show you a few places. I did some growing up here when I was your age." I wink.

"Oh, that would be fun. Can we go now?" She grips my hand and attempts to pull me off the bed.

Her eagerness is contagious. "Maybe not today. I'm a little tired from traveling, and isn't it close to dinnertime?"

Her shoulders slump. "Okay. Maybe after dinner then?"

"Only if your mom says it's okay," I say. She's a little pushy, this one, but I love her spirit.

She spins on her heel and leaves me to my bowl of emotions. It's a mix between anger over what I was deprived of and sadness that I couldn't see my sister and become her friend sooner. I wish I could have been here for her when she was growing up. Thankfully, she's at a very forgiving stage in life.

Things are going to be different now. I'm here, and I don't plan on going anywhere.

CHAPTER
Two

Charity

As I roll over, my stomach twists anxiously. Light gently filters into my room between the curtains. Today's the day I go back to college. After some full-on phone calls from Mom to the college, I'm finally allowed in.

The thought of coming face to face with people from my past is terrifying. The Charity they remember isn't the same one that left. Then there's Jase, my old best friend. Does he still live here? It probably doesn't matter. I was nine, and I'm sure whatever kind of friendship we had is long forgotten.

My phone vibrates on the nightstand. "Hello?" I answer.

"Hello, is this Charity?" An unfamiliar male voice comes through the line.

Sitting, I say, "Yes, it is. Can I ask who's calling?" I glance at the clock on the wall; it's eight in the morning. Who'd call this early?

"I'm Marcus, calling from Jacob and Son's law firm. It's to do with your father's will."

My stomach clenches. "Oh, okay. What's wrong?"

"No, nothing. We need to arrange a time we can get together. As I'm sure you're aware, your father left you with everything. Things need to happen with the house you both were occupying. I understand you have moved in with your mom?"

"Yes. I don't want to live in that house."

"I understand." His tone tells me he doesn't, though.

I sigh. "I wanted to get to know my mom and the family I have left that my father kept from me. Please forgive my bluntness, but I don't have the time to travel at the moment. I'll organize people to pack the house up and put it on the market." It's been a week since my arrival. I didn't *need* to come to live with my mom, but I wanted to. I am nineteen, after all. I wanted to get to know her; she's been a missing piece in my life. I'd sought her out. I needed someone. Growing up, my father kept a close rein on me, and my friends were limited, even at eighteen almost nineteen. School and home were all that was allowed.

Marcus clears his throat. "I'm sorry. Okay, well, when would be a good time for me to go through everything with you?"

"Now, because I don't want this hanging over my head as I wait for your call to come. What do I need to know that I don't already?" I snap. What a way to start my morning.

"Okay, so, your father obviously left you the house, his car—pretty much everything." I hear papers shuffle then he speaks again. "Did you have someone to handle things here, or would you like us to deal with the sale of the house and all the furniture? Your father has accounted for us taking care of it all; whatever it is you want to do."

"Fine. You take care of it. I'll email you my address to ship things. I also want the car sold. Sell every bit of furniture in the house. I only want the photos and letters that might be lying around. Get rid of all the plates, pots and pans—all of it. I don't need it. I would like everything from my bedroom shipped here. The bed, bedding, desk—you name it. Anything in that room, I want to be brought to me."

There's silence for a brief second before Marcus says, "All right. I have that all written down. I'll get things happening, and I'll be in touch if there's anything I need from you. Please email me your new address."

I scribble down his email address and end the call.

A knock on the door pulls me from the anger that I'm dwelling on. "Yeah?" I call.

"Is everything alright? You sounded angry." Mom steps into my room.

I sigh, rubbing my forehead. "Yeah, everything is okay. It was Dad's lawyers. They're taking care of everything for me, shipping me all the smaller stuff and anything else I want. I'm selling all the furniture and the house and the car. I've got them bringing all of my bedroom furniture, though. I hope that's okay."

Mom reaches out and takes my hand. The warmth surprises me. I've never known this compassion. "Charity, I'm happy to take you back to sort everything out if that's what you want, and if you want anything brought here, that's fine. This is your home as well." She squeezes my fingers.

I shake my head. "No, I'm done with that place." If she knew all the details, I'm not sure she'd want me to go back either.

"Okay. I'm here if you ever want to talk. Get ready and come down for breakfast. You've got a big day today." She gives my hand one more squeeze, and I feel it right in my heart.

I want to open up to her, to tell her everything. It's hard to do that; I have no idea where to begin. Being here with all of them has been some of the best days of my life over the last ten years. Why the hell did I stay where I was? I should have packed my bags and left. Oh, that's right. Dad liked to tell me no one would ever want me.

Standing in front of the mirror, I overthink what I'm wearing. I shouldn't care. My father always told me if something wasn't appropriate. "*Skirts are for ladies,*" he would say on numerous occasions. I'd then go and get out of my comfy jeans and pull on an ankle-length skirt or dress. I'm wearing dark-blue jeans that I've never been able to wear. I'd had them tucked away in the back of my cupboard so *he* wouldn't find them and throw them out.

"Wow, you look pretty." Grace stands at my doorway. She moves like a ninja, this girl.

Running my hands over my simple white tee, I say, "It's nothing crazy. Just casual."

She shrugs. "Still looks good."

Turning around, I take in her outfit. She's dressed in bright-pink tights with a light-pink tutu. "You're the one who looks good. Do you have a dance class before school?"

"Nope, this is what I'm wearing to school." She sways her tutu from side to side.

A smile tugs at my lips. "Well, you look beautiful. I might need to take some styling tips from you."

She giggles and runs out of the room.

I turn back to the unfamiliar girl in the mirror. This is the new me. New Charity. Look out, world; there's no holding me back now.

After tying my hair up in a simple messy bun and applying some foundation, eyeliner, and mascara, I make my way downstairs. The smell of bacon makes my mouth water and stomach growl at the same time.

Voices talk in hushed tones as I step around the corner into the dining room, which is across from the kitchen. Paul, my mother's husband, and Mom stand close together. I take her in as she turns some frying bacon. Her long locks are tied up in a similar messy bun to mine. Fitted white jeans hug her curves, and she also wears a light-pink top. A floral apron hangs over her neck and is tied around her waist. She's definitely not a Stepford wife, but she is beautiful.

"Good morning," I greet them both, even though I've already spoken to Mom this morning. I'm choosing to ignore their private conversation, which suddenly stopped the moment I came into the room.

"Good morning," they say in sync.

Mom rushes over and puts some plates on the table, along with some orange juice and milk. A squeal behind me alerts me to a chubby-cheeked boy running right for my legs.

"Stop him, Charity. He's got jam all over his face," Mom yells. I catch him just before he gets the chance to smear his breakfast all over my new pants and white top.

I pick him up and put him in his highchair. "Look at you, you little grub. Are you trying to force me to change before I leave?" I coo. The smile on his face makes my heart soar.

This kid has ways of having everyone wrapped around his little fingers.

"Yes," Beau says proudly.

"He's quick," Mom says as she places a plate on the highchair with another piece of toast.

"Yes, he is," I agree.

Gesturing to the table set with a pile of food, Mom says, "Help yourself to whatever you feel like. Do you want a lift to school, or would you like to walk? It's only two blocks away if you remember."

"I'll just walk if that's okay."

"Not a problem."

After I finish a filling breakfast, Mom hands me a bag. "This has everything you need. Paul and I got you a laptop."

"Oh, you didn't need to do that. I would have gotten one once everything was finalized with Dad's stuff." I glance down at the bag and then back to her. "Thank you," I choke out.

Mom wraps her arms around me, and it's like her love fills me with such emotion that it overflows. Tears brim my eyes as she holds me tightly. I haven't let her get close enough to hug me. I knew this would happen. Dad told me that big girls don't cry.

I jerk back from Mom as though my father's words have slapped me across the face.

"Sorry. I'll see you after. Thank you again." I swallow down the lump in my throat and wipe away any evidence of my tears. Mom's eyes shine with concern. If only she knew the half of how destroyed I am inside.

Tears are for the weak.

CHAPTER
Three

Charity

The streets and houses are the exact same as I remember them from when I'd walk to school with Mom when I was younger. A memory captures me as I see the very familiar ice cream cart on the corner. My father stopped there every day on our way home when he'd collect me from school. Jase had been with me. He'd treat us both to whatever we wanted. My heart clenches at the happy memory.

The sun beats down on my skin, darkening it. My mother has a beautiful complexion I wish I'd inherited. Maybe because my life has been largely spent indoors, and I've never had the chance to bathe in the sunlight. The sun's rays are like a drug I want more of. I want more freedom—something I've not experienced in a long time.

I'm not sure what Dad's aim was in keeping me locked away from the world. I'd always thought it was normal until I was sixteen. My friends would invite me places, and Dad's answer was forever the same—*no*. One night, I pushed and pushed to the point where he literally shoved me into the wall. I never spoke to him like that again. I saw the raging flame in his dark, haunting eyes. If I'd kept going, I'm not sure what would have happened. He wasn't the man he was when I was younger.

Surely, though, he cared about me. He had to. He wouldn't have treated me how he did if he didn't care about me and want to keep me safe. Yes, that was it. He cared. A hard pain punches me right in the chest at the thought of doubting Dad. There are reasons for everything. Things happen because they are supposed to.

Lost in my thoughts, I hadn't realized the college campus was now in view. The large, dark brick buildings with a shining green lawn. Panic claws at my chest. Panic at the thought of running into those familiar faces that surely are going to have questions which I'm not willing to share the answers to.

Just make it through the first class, and the rest will be easier, I remind myself. I can do the hard things.

So many faces turn my way as I enter the campus quad. *One foot in front of the other. Keep going.* I make a beeline for the entrance doors, my eyes focused on them. The hustle and bustle of the corridor has me looking around in amazement. I've always been at home, gone to school, and then gone home again. There was no mingling—Dad's rules. He's no longer here. I can actually hang out with any friends I make. Actual real friends. People to talk to. No one is here to hold me back now.

An unfamiliar face stalks past me with a furrowed brow. I smile. He looks at me, puzzled, but keeps walking. I don't care. I'm free of the man who held me back, and I plan to live the life that's intended for me.

Turning my head around the room, I drink up the atmosphere. It's buzzing, electric even. My skin tingles with excitement. Not paying attention to where I'm going, I collide with a large body. I fall back, landing flat on my ass, a throbbing pain taking up residence in my butt cheek.

"I'm so sorry." I scurry to get up, dusting the imaginary dust from my clothes. A large hand takes hold of my arm, helping me up then releasing me. "Sorry again, I didn't see you there."

Slowly, my eyes connect to those of the person I collided with.

Of course it would be him.

"Charity? Is that you?"

My head spins as I stare at the older yet familiar face of Jase, the boy I had a major crush on when I was younger. I'd thought for sure he would have tried to contact me. We were connected at the hip.

He has changed so much from how I remember him. He's no longer this scrawny little boy with messy blond hair. Well, the messy hair is still the same, but it suits him so much better now. My heart is pounding in my ears. That's totally not normal. Why does it have to be him I run into the minute I step foot into this place?

Jase's stare holds me hostage. I keep my gaze trained on those blue eyes, clear and questioning.

"Ah, yeah. It's me. Who are you?" I stand a little taller and give a teasing smile. Of course I know who he is, but I'd like to see how he feels when he's forgotten.

"Surely you remember me." He laughs while running his fingers through his blond locks. "You're really here, aren't you? I'm not imagining it?" He chuckles. He reaches out and takes my arm again. His warmth wraps itself around my arm and spreads quickly. "It's you," he says breathlessly. That's exactly how I'm feeling—breathless.

I move and pull my arm from his grip, then I say, "Yeah, it's really me. I'm back. Still not sure who you are, though." I shrug. The heat in my cheeks becomes stronger. I shouldn't be embarrassed in front of Jase. He was my friend long before my father took me away, yet he never tried to reach out to me like he said he would. I'd given letters to my dad to post. Did he ever send them, though? "Anyway, I have to get to class. See you later." *Or not.*

I nod and step around him, feeling somewhat stupid over this whole encounter.

As I settle into my first class, I can't focus on what the teacher standing before me is saying. I should be paying attention given the fact that I've already missed so much school, considering it's partway into the semester. Jase's touch still lingers like it's been etched into my skin. So unforgettable.

He was the one person I could rely on. He's in all my memories from as far back as I can remember. We would write notes to each other and stick them in each other's letterbox. He lived seven houses up from me, and now I've come back. My phone vibrates in my pocket. I pull it out and open the message.

> **Mom:** Hey, honey, just wanted to check in and see how your day is going.

I've never had these nice messages or been checked up on. I've always had texts that read "You should be home by now" or that featured something more aggressive. I type a quick reply.

Charity: Hey, yeah everything's going well.

Mom: I'm so glad to hear that. Well, call me if you need anything. We still have to go shopping to pick out some things for your bedroom. I know you have things coming from your home, but maybe we can update other items if you want. Have a think about what you'd like. See you this afternoon.

I don't reply. Instead, I stare at her words. She is my mother. She actually does care about me. This feeling is foreign; I've not experienced motherly love in a long time. My chest swells at this new sensation spreading through me.

"Nice of you to join us, Miss Kent," the teacher's droney voice says, which pulls my attention to the person he's addressing. I can't even remember his name. My eyes go wide when I see who's walking to a chair. Paislee. Isn't today a walk down Memory Lane? I remember our little pretend tea parties in our backyard on a picnic blanket. My lips tug up on one side. Shaking my head, I'm unable to hide the grin that grows on my face.

She's stopped, and her mouth hangs open, her eyes on me.

"Excuse me, Miss Kent. Are you having trouble locating your seat?" the teacher asks.

Her mouth shuts, and her head shakes as she starts walking again, this time heading right for the empty chair beside mine.

Even as she takes a seat, her focus doesn't shift. Dropping her bag to the floor, she faces me. My bottom lip finds its way between my teeth, and I chomp down on it.

Her analyzing gaze has me shifting uncomfortably. Without saying anything, she pokes me in the arm. My hand comes up and covers the spot she touched.

"Charity, please tell me I haven't lost my mind and that you're actually sitting here in my class," she whispers.

I chuckle quietly so the teacher doesn't hear. Although, I'm sure he's that ancient he'd have to turn up his hearing aid to hear me. "What's with everyone actually touching me? Actually, let's pretend I'm a ghost, come back to haunt you." Reaching out, I poke her in the arm. A loud gasp escapes her throat.

"Excuse me, ladies, can we continue this conversation after class?"

Both our heads flick toward the teacher who glowers in our direction.

Paislee's hand reaches out and covers mine where it rests over the top of my books. I glance over. "I'm so happy you're here," she whispers then removes her hand. I'm not mad at her; she never made the promise to keep in touch. Jase did.

The rest of class is a blur. First Jase, my old best friend, and now Paislee, the girl who was like a sister to me. I wonder what they think now that I'm back. Do they know about my dad? Jase's piercing blue eyes flash in my mind. What would he think of the girl I've become over the years? Perhaps it's best for me to keep my distance. One thing I know is that when you unsettle the past, it tends to come at you like a steamroller, and before you realize it, it's caused you pain.

CHAPTER
Four

Jase

I t was her. I still can't believe it. She is real, and damn, has she become gorgeous. Her hair is long, dark, and thick. My fingers itched to run through it when I saw her. And her piercing green eyes held me captive. But why did she act like she didn't know who I was?

"Yo, dude, pay attention," Blane shouts as he tosses the football in my direction. I snap back to attention. We stand on the football field, tossing the ball, and my fingers curl easily around the ball, catching it. "What's got you love drunk and not paying attention? I've only seen you this unfocused when you were preparing to take that Paislee girl out on a date. Now look at how that turned out. You were friend-zoned once again."

If I were standing near him, I'd probably jab him in the rib for that remark. "Shut up, man."

Blane is our star quarterback. The only problem with him is that he doesn't have a damn filter on that mouth of his.

He laughs as we continue to toss the football. "Where's your head at if it's not here? You realize the coach will tear into you if you're unfocused, and then we'll all be running laps of the field, so speak."

I sigh as the ball leaves my hand again. "I ran into someone I haven't seen in...I think it's been close to ten years. She was my best friend when we were younger. I guess I'm a little surprised to see her. She moved away with her dad. I swear, he wasn't all there in the head. I remember how destroyed her mom was when they left. We would go over and console her. She tried everything to get her back, but her husband was a piece of work—from what I remember, anyway."

Blane pauses. "Would I remember her?"

Shaking my head, I say, "No. This was before you moved to town. I really thought she would never come back. Yet, there she was in the hall today."

"Damn, man. That's got to be a shock. So, what are you going to do about it?"

I shrug. "I have no idea. She acted as though she didn't know who I was. We're completely different people now. For all I know, she'll want nothing to do with me. Perhaps that's why she doesn't remember me—that's if she's telling me the truth. I never heard from her again, even though I gave her my address. We exchanged addresses. We were going to write and keep in contact."

"Oh well, doesn't matter. I'm sure you'll be friend-zoned with her too." He laughs. "Hey, when is your brother coming in? Coach said we'll be getting a visit from him."

Oh, the big superstar pro-football-player older brother. The athletic gene seems to run in our family—or maybe it's just how much Dad pushes us.

"I'm not sure. Lachlan will probably show up when it suits him. You know him and how he is. All this fame and money has gone to his head," I say, shrugging.

"Ha, yeah, that's true. It's good for you, though; you have an in into the pros."

"Yeah," I reply without much enthusiasm. Can't say it's high on my priority list at the moment. Of course, I enjoy the sport, but the pressure to perform the best I can is sometimes overwhelming. "We better hit the gym with the rest of the team, or they'll think we slacked off." Walking off the field, I grab my bag from the green grass, Blane following closely behind.

"What are you going to do about your woman?"

Without thinking, I backhand him in the stomach. He coughs and crouches over to catch his breath.

"She's not my woman," I practically growl. We're nothing. I want to talk to her again, though it seems as if she plans on giving me a wide berth. A lot can change in ten years. I wonder if she's still the same warm, funny girl I remember.

Getting to know her and who she is now has suddenly become my number-one priority.

Who is Charity? What happened to her over the years?

CHAPTER
Five

Charity

"Where have you been hiding, girl? What are you doing here? Just visiting?" Paislee's questions come at me at a million miles an hour. My hands hug the mug of coffee that's just been placed in front of me.

After class, Paislee all but dragged me to the campus cafe and forced me into a booth, and now I'm being questioned as though it's an interrogation. Tension in my stomach pulls tighter with each question. I shouldn't feel this anxious over talking to an old friend.

Releasing my mug, I hold my hands up. "Whoa, settle down on the questions there. Let's start with the first one. I moved away with Dad, as I'm sure you remember. He passed away recently, which has now drawn me back here to try and build a relationship with Mom. So, no, I'm not visiting. I'm here permanently." I suck in a breath after offloading that buttload of information.

Paislee's hands go to her now open mouth. "I'm so sorry about your dad." If only she knew how much better off I really was, she wouldn't be.

"It's all right. I'm happy to be back here, though. I think. It's a little surreal. So many familiar faces already, and yet, I'm still the outsider." I laugh. That's what I am and always have been. On my own. I've kept to my own thoughts. I'm surprised they haven't sent me mad by now.

Paislee shoves my shoulder across the table. "Stop thinking like that. You've got me now. Although, we don't normally do tea parties anymore. I like *actual* parties with boys, alcohol, and dancing."

We laugh together.

"I never got the chance to go to those kinds of parties. It's always been about getting good grades." Lifting the warm drink, I take a sip, the heat washing through me.

"That's all going to change now that we've caught up. I'll give you my number; hand me your phone."

After digging my cell from the pocket of my bag, I hand it to her. She quickly puts her number in and hands it back.

"There, and I've sent myself a message so I have your number as well."

The door chimes, and Paislee's face lights up like a girl in love. She waves someone over.

Turning, I spot a very good-looking guy coming in our direction. He takes a seat on her side of the table. They kiss, and then his attention is back to me. His grin is heart-stopping. "Charity, this is my boyfriend, Dane. Dane, this is my old friend, Charity, who has just moved back to town," she says with a giant smile. This guy has won her heart.

Dane extends his hand. I take it. "Nice to meet you," he says.

"Yeah, you too." I take my hand back, and Paislee takes over the conversation again.

"Alright, this weekend we're hitting a party. You okay with that?" She rubs her hands together as though she's concocting something.

"I haven't ever been to a party," I admit, my voice barely a whisper and muffled by my mug.

"What was that?" Paislee asks.

Swallowing my mouthful of coffee, I say, "I've never been to a college party—or any party, for that matter." It feels weird admitting that to her and her boyfriend, considering I've never admitted anything like that to anyone.

"Hello." Paislee snaps her fingers in my face.

Shaking my head, I say, "Sorry, got caught in my thoughts."

"It's okay. Do you want me to come to your place to help you get ready this weekend?"

"I'd really appreciate that. I probably need some new clothes if I'm being honest." I give a small grin, and at the same time, her face lights up and Dane groans.

"Don't give her the shopping power. She'll make you spend more than you want to." If only he knew I needed a whole new wardrobe. No more skirts for this girl.

"That's okay. I'm going to need all the help I can get."

Paislee claps excitedly. "Perfect! I'll get the girls together, and we can go shopping on Thursday. Are you okay with that?"

I nod as excitement rushes through me. I'm going shopping with *friends*. Goodness, if I said half this stuff out loud, they'd probably think I'm some crazy girl.

New life. New me.

Stepping through the door, Mom yells for Grace, and Beau is screaming—and not in a good way. It pierces my ears. Placing my bags down, I go looking for my brother.

"Beau, where are you, little man?" I call. He steps out from behind the couch, his face red and blotchy with tears still streaming down his rosy cheeks. "Hey, what's wrong?" I step toward him with my arms open, and he runs into them. Lifting his little body, I rest him on my hip and go in search of her. "Mom?"

"In the bathroom," she calls back.

Turning to Beau, I say, "Come on." He snuggles his face into my neck, his little hiccup sniffles slowly subsiding.

I enter the bathroom then stop in my tracks. Drops of blood paint the floor, and Mom is fussing over Grace.

"What happened?" I'm unable to hide the shock in my voice.

Mom presses a washcloth to Grace's head and turns to me. Her face is flushed. She sighs. "This is what happens when a toddler hits his sister in the head with a toy truck that is supposed to be outside." She sighs again and gives Beau a stern mother's look. He nuzzles deeper into my neck.

"Oh, dear. Are you okay, Gracie?" I ask.

She sniffles. "Yes, it's okay." A sob escapes her.

"I'll take Beau for a walk if you want?"

Mom's eyes meet mine, and she smiles. "I'd really appreciate you doing that. Thank you."

After grabbing some snacks and placing Beau into the stroller, I head for the park down the road. There's a great playground there for the kids. Well, that's what Grace has told me. I've still yet to bring her here. I've been too caught up in my own head to actually take in some things. It was like today in class. Everything went by in a blur. I don't remember the lessons or what I need to do.

"Og, og," Beau shouts and points to a dog and its owner, walking down the opposite side of the street.

"That's right. Dog," I say.

After arriving at the park, I take Beau from the stroller and let him run off. I keep a close eye on him; I'd hate for something to happen to him on my watch. My gaze shifts over the playground and field beside it. Little boys and girls run, squeal, jump, and skip over the equipment and chase balls in the field.

"Charity?"

I freeze. Him again. Twice in one day. *Jase.*

Shifting on the bench, I turn to face him. A red ball cap covers his blond hair, but once again, those eyes do something to my insides. They dance. "Oh, it's you," I say politely, adding in a smile.

He gestures to the seat. "Do you mind if I sit with you?"

My hands tremble in my lap, but I turn my attention back to Beau who is sliding down a slide. "Ah, sure, if you want. It's a free world."

He chuckles, taking a seat beside me, but he's sure to keep some space between us. He's so huge, a hulky figure— his entire body is pure muscle. And those arms. Damn, don't even get me started. I take in his outfit: black running shorts and an orange tee. His arms are way too big for the sleeves. A grin tugs at my lips at the thought.

He screams *sexy, hot,* and *every girl's fantasy.* One heated look from him and women would be fainting at his feet. My heart races triple its regular rate.

"Are you looking for a quick getaway?"

I snap my head to face him, my eyes wide. "What? No. I was simply checking the time. Are you stalking me?" I cock an eyebrow.

His mouth twitches then he says, "No, I was heading out for a run and caught sight of you. I wanted to talk." He pauses a moment before saying, "Do you really not remember me?"

I turn my attention back to Beau, who seems to have made friends with another little boy. They're running around, holding hands, laughing, and they climb up the slide, and he follows his new friend. *Do I tell him the truth?* Swallowing my pride, I decide it's better to do the right thing than lie. I'm not my father. "Of course I remember you." I sigh.

"Then why did you act like you didn't know me?"

I close my eyes. I was hoping to avoid this line of questioning a bit longer. Yet, here we are. I could simply walk away, but I won't.

We shift and face each other. I soak up the calm aroma that emanates from him. I catch his hand flexing open and shut. Could he be just as nervous as I am over this conversation?

Biting the bullet, I finally say, "It doesn't feel good being forgotten, does it?" The words are like venom dripping from my tongue. His head draws back. Those electric-blue eyes darken a little.

Shaking his head, he holds up his hands. "Wait, what? You're the one who dropped off the face of the earth."

"Pfft. Do you really think I would have wanted to go with my dad if I had known what my life would have been like living under his roof?" I snap.

"What do you mean? Did something happen?" He reaches for me, and I rear back from his touch. I don't deserve it or want it. I'm damaged, broken. I'm not about to tell Jase that, though; I don't want his or anyone else's pity.

I stand abruptly. Jase follows my movements.

"No," I lie. "It's not your concern. *I'm* not your concern. You decided a long time ago that I wasn't worth your time and forgot me."

"No, that's not right. I—"

"Just stop," I cut him off, my voice raising a little, and I can't hide the shake to my words. "Jase, please don't." I hold my hand up. "Now isn't the time. I don't want to delve into my life over the last ten years. I'm not ready for that."

"Harity, I hungry." Beau's little voice pulls me back from the dark road I was beginning to walk down.

"Okay, buddy, here's some fruit." After picking him up, I put him in his stroller and hand him the pieces of apple I'd chopped up for him. "Hey, Ase." My hands freeze as I realize Beau knows Jase. It doesn't stop the laugh; it sounded like he just called Jase an ass.

He chuckles. "Hey, Beau. How are those apples?"

"Good," Beau says clearly.

I face Jase again. The grin on his face is wicked, yet it draws me in. I'm sure he gets whoever and whenever he wants. "You two old friends?" I ask.

He shrugs. "You could say that. We've played at the park a few times. I'll be running some laps, and he'll join me."

"Isn't there a campus field for that?"

"Yeah, but sometimes getting away from that place is good for the soul. Especially the soul that already has so much pressure thrust upon it."

"You? Pressure? Yeah, right. I'm sure you're the golden boy on campus."

He shuffles his feet. "It's not like I asked for that. I can't help that my brother made it to the pros with his football career, and now everyone expects the same of me. But that's a story for another time. Perhaps I'll share my story when you're ready to talk to me about what happened to you over the years."

I take an apple from Beau and pop it in my mouth with a crunch. "That's not going to happen anytime soon." Hopefully, not ever.

"Well, can we start over? Friends?" He holds out his hand, and I take it.

"Friends." I smile, but trepidation lurches in my stomach.

How do I stop myself from falling for him now? It was easier being mad at him.

CHAPTER Six

Jase

That smile—I'm not so sure it's genuine. There's pain hidden behind it, and as much as I want to probe and get all the answers, it's not going to be an easy task.

"Well, I better get going. I'm meeting a friend shortly," I say. Paislee is going to kill me for being late, but I'm sure once I tell her why, she'll understand.

"Yeah. I'll see you around." Charity's back is turned to me. She's closed off and hard to reach. What did she go through?

Deciding it's better to leave than push her, I reluctantly jog off. It was a coincidence that I'd caught her here. I was ready to talk to her tomorrow about everything, but judging by how that just went, it's going to take more than one conversation to knock down the walls she's clearly put up.

I catch Paislee waiting for me at the end of the street. She's dressed in her runners, tights, and one of Dane's shirts. I swear she wears his clothes more than her own.

"You do realize you're late?" she snaps while tapping her watch.

"I know, I know. I ran into a friend. Sorry." This has become a routine of ours of late. At least three times a week, we jog together. Usually, it ends with her finishing early, and I keep going on my own.

"Speaking of friends, I ran into an old one of mine today. I think she'd be perfect for you. I want to set you up on a blind date." She winks before taking off down the side street. With my long strides, it doesn't take much to catch up to her.

"I'm not into blind dates; they always end in disaster." We match pace. I slow mine so she can keep up with me.

"Come on, trust me. This is one that will end well. It has to," she puffs out.

"Who is it?"

"I'm not telling you. It wouldn't be a blind date if I did." She slaps me on the arm.

"I must not be the dating kind of guy; I don't seem to be right for anyone. Every girl I date always wants only one thing, and I'm not *that* guy, as much as people may think I am." I take some breaths and concentrate on the pavement.

Paislee is silent. I'm beginning to wonder if this is where she's going to bail on me. She slows to a walk, and I follow suit. "You have to stop thinking like that. You're not that guy. I know it. But you allow yourself to be shoved into the friend zone corner. How about you start fighting for whoever it is you want." She shrugs.

She's right. How do I make that work for me, though? "Maybe I'm just not meeting the right girls."

"That's a possibility as well."

"Hey, how would I get a girl who has built a wall to open up to me?" I ask.

Paislee's face turns. "What do you mean? You want help getting her to open up to you?"

"Yeah. She's very closed off. Hard to talk to."

"How well do you know this girl?"

I shrug. Not really at all anymore. I'm not going to tell her that, though. "Only a little."

"Who is she?"

"I'm not telling you since you won't tell me who you plan to set me up on a date with." I waggle my eyebrows teasingly.

"You're no fun. But in answer to your question, I guess you just have to keep trying with this girl. If you give up, then she isn't going to come to you. Show her you care. That you're there for her," Paislee says and then takes off at a sprint. I give her a moment to get ahead a little and then go after her.

Giving Charity the space she needs seems like a better idea, but I see what Paislee is meaning. Trying is better than not. I want Charity to talk to me, to let me back into her life.

When I finally get home, the sun has completely set. The familiar black truck in the driveway of the football house causes me to groan.

"Damn. Not the man I want to see tonight," I mutter. Hearing his voice causes a rush of anger to flare inside my chest. I drag my feet to the front door and begrudgingly push my way through.

"Jase, son, where have you been?" He stalks toward me. I stand taller than my father, but of course, he has me and

Lachlan, *his successful son,* bending over backwards to achieve the things he couldn't. Why do parents do this kind of thing to their kids? Always pushing them to do what they couldn't.

I drop my gaze to my runners then glance back up at him. "What does it look like I've been doing?" I gesture to myself.

"Don't be a smart mouth, son. Why weren't you at training today?"

Here we go.

"I had schoolwork to finish. If I don't do my work, I can't actually play on the team, so schoolwork comes first sometimes," I say, stepping around him.

"Training and football are priorities for you, Jase. We've spoken about this."

I roll my eyes as I walk past Blane, who appears to be working on his laptop with headphones on. He's totally listening in. At least he doesn't have a father like mine who demands everything be his way.

After grabbing a bottle of water from the fridge, I twist the cap and swallow two mouthfuls before speaking again. "Dad, I understand what you want. What if football isn't what I want?"

Blane's head shoots up, his eyes wide. I knew that would grab his attention.

Dad rubs the bridge of his nose then turns his glare on me. "Your mother and I have put everything into our boys. Why do you have to be so defiant? We're not asking much. Look at Lachlan; he's got a great career and is succeeding. We want the same for you."

If only he knew how much screwing around Lachlan actually did. It's only a matter of time before he messes something up, and then Dad's attention will be turned on him again.

"I know what you and Mom want. You want two golden boys who bring in the money for you, achieving the dreams you never could," I say through gritted teeth. I don't want to deal with him and his constant pushing. The more pushing he does, the more I want to pull away from it all.

Dad crosses his arms over his broad chest, resting them on his slight beer belly. "I'm sorry you feel that way." He turns his back to me and walks out. I cringe as he slams the door. A sigh escapes me.

"Is that true? You don't want to play? I thought for sure you would live and breathe football," Blane says, placing his headphones down and eyeing me with skepticism.

"Don't get me wrong. I enjoy the game, and perhaps I do want to go pro, but I want to do it because it's what I want—not what the man in the suit wants. I saw how much he rode Lachlan. Now it's my turn, and I'm not going to let him walk all over me."

"Gee, tense much?" Blane teases, laughing. "You need to find yourself a woman to take away some of this tension that's rolling off you."

After finishing my water, I screw the lid back on and toss the bottle at him. "Shut up. I'm heading for a shower. Order some food."

"You got it, Cap." He salutes me. Rolling my eyes, I walk away. Perhaps he's right about the finding-a-woman thing.

Pulling my cell from my armband, I shoot a message to Paislee.

Jase: Okay, I'll go on the blind date. What's her number?

CHAPTER
Seven

Charity

The last couple of days have flown by, and now I'm walking around a shop with some very out-there girls who want to try on every piece of clothing in the store. Paislee has brought her two friends with her: Addison, who is her brother's girlfriend, and Elsie. Apparently, she has an Australian boyfriend. I'd love to meet him—those accents are awesome.

I've been staring at this navy-blue dress covered in daisies. It's long and flowing. Mom gave me money to grab some things. I'm guessing she noticed the bags of clothes I tossed out yesterday after going through everything I own. Every single good-girl skirt I owned I put in the large black garbage bag, ready for Goodwill. I never want to see anything like those again. This dress is fitted to the waist, and then it drops to the floor. It's everything my father would go against. I love it.

"Oh, that is gorgeous. Are you going to get it?" Addison asks while she reaches out and touches the fabric. I take the one in my size from the rack.

"Yeah, I really like it," I say while grinning at the piece of fabric that's bringing me new joy.

"You should see these cute shirts," Paislee calls from another section in the clothing store. Slowly, I make my way to where she is and soak up all the other pieces of clothing along the way. I really want more jeans and some shorts, because I don't have any.

When I finally find her, she's holding a stunning satin, light-pink top with lace covering the shoulders.

"Wow, it's beautiful," I breathe as I take it from her hands and check the size is right.

"That will be perfect for your blind date." She winks.

"What blind date? I didn't agree to anything of the sort."

Paislee groans. "Why not? It'll be fun. You can meet someone new and, who knows, maybe hit it off."

"I'm not so sure I want to," I say as I lay the top over the top on my arm, ready to take them to the register.

Paislee's hands shoot out and wrap around my arm. "Pllleeeease," she begs. "I can beg; I can go all night with this. Just give him one shot. I'll give you his number, and you can contact him, or would you like me to give him yours?"

Neither is preferable, is what I want to say. Instead, an image of my father flashes in my mind. I've been on lockdown for so long, and now is my time to shine. Screw all the rules my father implemented. He's not here anymore. "Fine. You get him to message me. At least then I won't feel like I'm pressuring him."

"Oh, he's keen; he's already told me so, and I've already given him your number. I can give him the go-ahead now." She claps excitedly. I'm too stunned to process what she just said. She's already given my number to him? Before I can say anything, she says, "Perfect! You'll hear from him." She pauses a moment and pulls her phone out. Her fingers move like lightning over the screen, and then she slips it away into her pocket and looks around the rest of the store. "Okay, girls, let's go to the next shop."

I pay for my items, and then we head to the next store. We stop to buy some donuts. "So, do you like being back here?" Paislee's friend Elsie asks. She's pretty blunt and says things how she sees them. I like people like that.

"Yeah, it's been good getting to know my mom again and the rest of her family."

"Don't you mean *your family?*" Elsie asks as she shoves a piece of donut in her mouth. Paislee shoves her in the arm. "Sorry," she mumbles.

"No, that's okay. You're right; they are my family. I'm just not used to calling them that. It's been so long that I'm not sure how to act around my mom, but my brother and sister are cute. I've never been more excited than I was the day I found out about them." There's always a positive to a negative, and I choose to take all I've gone through and turn it into something good—like getting to know my mom and siblings.

"That's cool. What was your dad like?" Addison asks, and this time, she gets a glare from Paislee.

Reaching out, I touch her arm. "It's okay. He was a good man." Even as I say the words, they form concrete in my throat. He was a great dad, but deep down in my stomach, I know there were things he did that weren't right.

"Anyway, I passed your number on, so you'll hear from your date soon." Paislee takes the chance to change the topic. One day, I'm going to have to address all the buried emotions caused by my father. I'm so torn over him and the kind of person he was.

"Who are you setting her up with?" Elsie asks.

"I'm not telling you. You'll go and say something stupid and blow all my hard work. Nope, this secret is staying with me and each party involved." She laughs.

"Well, I guess I better find a couple more outfits, considering I have been living in the same pair of jeans all week," I say with a small smile.

"Did your dad not buy you clothes? I mean, of course he did, but why the same pair of jeans?" Elsie pipes up, confusion evident in her tone.

"Yeah, he did. I just never got a say in what they looked like." I shrug and attempt to ignore all the eyes that are now on me. "Please don't stare. Let's go shopping."

It takes them a moment. Then we turn into another clothing store. My thoughts are still on my father.

"Elsie, where is my makeup?" Paislee calls from Addison's bedroom. I decided I wanted to get ready with them at Addison and Elsie's campus dorm. They do have another two girls living here, but they've gone away somewhere for a little while. Who goes away when school is on? People who obviously don't care about their future.

"I've got it out here," Elsie yells. Gee, the whole building could hear us, I'm sure of it.

Paislee fusses in front of me, holding an eye shadow pallet with a rainbow of colors I'd never consider putting on myself. She hovers her brush over one and then shifts to another. It's easier if I shut my eyes; that way I'm not stressing over what tones and colors she's using. She jumps up and races off, my eyes spring open, and then she's back with a case of I-don't-know-what, and I'm a little afraid to ask. She clicks it open, revealing more makeup. I didn't take her for the full-on makeup type. Elsie, on the other hand, I did.

"Wow, please don't make me look like a clown. I still remember the terrible job you did to me when we were kids." I laugh.

She opens a few more palettes and finally settles on one that's full of neutral colors. "Girl, I've got you. You're going to look stunning. These parties are fun, and I want you to have a good time. I'm not going to do yours like mine, unless you want me to?"

Her eyes have a smoky effect applied to them, with shimmering eyeliner along the top and bottom of her eyelids. Her bright-red lips open slightly as she picks up a brush and then tosses it back down and chooses another, finally happy with it.

Feeling adventurous, I say, "Can we go a little crazy tonight? I've never been done up like you are."

Paislee grins. "Yes, let's go crazy."

"Yeah."

Thirty minutes later, I'm standing in front of the full-length mirror in the bedroom. My eyes soak up every part of me—a *new* me. I like this girl staring back at me. She looks confident and happy. "Wow, I look…"

"You look stunning. That pink shirt was the right choice, and those jeans work wonders for your already amazing figure." Paislee wraps her arm around my shoulders and pulls me tight against her. Emotions swell through me, causing a lump to form in my throat. "What's wrong? You don't like it? I can tone the makeup down if you want."

My head shakes before she even finishes her sentence. "No. I'm just... thank you so much," I breathe, turning to face her. "I feel so alive. A new me. Thank you for taking me in and making me feel welcome." Tears fill my eyes.

"No, no, don't cry. Let's not mess up that beautiful face with tears." Paislee turns and grabs a tissue from the bed. "Here, tilt your head and rest this just in the corners of your eyes to soak up the tears before they fall. I've had to do this plenty of times."

Doing as she says, I remain silent, feeling a little stupid over my slight meltdown. "Sorry, Pais."

"Girl, you have nothing to be sorry about. If anything, I should be the one who is sorry for not trying to contact you. We were best friends. I know friends grow apart, but you were like my sister. I shouldn't have let you walk away and done nothing." She pulls me into her tight embrace. It's as though no time has passed between us.

We stand together for a short time. When everything feels settled, she releases me, and I'm feeling so much better. I brush my hands down my outfit and then bring them back up and meet Paislee's smile. "Thanks for helping me get ready."

"It's only the beginning, Charity. We've got plenty more parties to attend and time together. The next few years are going to be epic for us." She shrugs.

"I can't afford it right now. Why don't you live on campus?"

"Nah, I'm cheap." She laughs. "Mom does so much for me, and I'd hate for her to be alone in her big house, although I'm sure she hasn't been alone sometimes—especially since my Dad came back onto the scene."

This is a shock. "Your dad came back?"

She nods. "Yeah, and he's been getting to know Parker and I, and I'm noticing he's actually spending more time with Mom. Not sure how I feel about that, though. So long as she's happy, then so am I."

"Hurry up, you pair," Elsie shouts from the living area.

Paislee rolls her eyes. "Here we go. I'll keep an eye on you, as will the boys. You're in good hands. If at any time you don't feel comfortable, let me know. I've got you."

I nod, and she grips my hand and drags me out to the others.

"Damn, you look amazing!" Elsie says with a huge grin plastered on her face.

"You look like a completely different person," Addison adds. She's right; I'm not the same girl who moved back to town a couple of weeks ago, and it's exciting to let go of all the rules that were forced upon me for so long. Look out, world—new Charity is here.

CHAPTER
Eight

Jase

"Dude, that was an epic game." Some guy holds out his hand. I take it, and we bump shoulders.

"Thanks, man. Have a good night." Giving him a swift nod, I step around him. The house is slowly starting to fill. We won our game tonight, and we're celebrating the right way—with a party. It wouldn't be college life if there weren't parties every other weekend.

Dane, Parker, Aiden, and Jimmy spot me and make their way over. I quickly scan the room to see if their girls are here. Will Charity come with them?

"Hey, man," Parker greets me with a clap of hands and bump of shoulders again. "You did good."

"Thanks. It was pretty rough out there tonight. That team seemed to be made of concrete." I laugh.

"Yeah, it looked like it," Dane chimes in.

"Oh look, the girls' brigade has finally arrived. Fashionably late, as always. And who is this new one that's joined?" Aiden asks with a laugh.

My heart skips a beat when I glance behind me. Charity has ripped my breath from my lungs. Her jeans hug her long legs, and as I trail my gaze up her body, I soak up each movement she makes. Her hair hangs down over her shoulders. Light waves of it bounce as she walks. Paislee has her arm hooked through Charity's. When Charity's face comes up, it doesn't even look like her. Paislee has been at her with the makeup. But she was already beautiful.

"Who's their friend?" Jimmy asks. A glint of I-don't-know-what shines in his eyes. The ugly green monster takes a seat on my shoulder. I instantly want to protect her from him. He's always been a moody person. From what I've heard, he's also not nice. I'm surprised he's with these guys. But they obviously know him more than what I do, and I can't take what I hear as something solid until I've witnessed it.

"That's Charity. She lived here years ago and has just moved back to town," Parker says. "Pais and her were friends before."

"She's a looker," Aiden says. My gaze shifts to him, and he meets my glare. His eyebrows shoot up, and then a massive grin slides across his face. "Okay, okay," he says in a low voice so only I can hear him. Perhaps my stare gave away more than I intended it to.

"Hey, boys," Paislee greets us. Her words are smooth, and she releases Charity and steps up to Dane, planting a kiss on his lips.

"Enough of that in front of me," Parker groans. That would be hard—your best friend dating your little sister. Glad I only have a brother. Though that comes with its own problems.

"Guys, this is Charity. Charity, this is Aiden, Parker, Jimmy, and of course you know Jase. You already met Dane." Paislee goes around the circle, pointing to everyone else. When she lands on me, her grin snaps to wicked. What has she got planned?

"Hey, everyone," Charity says. Her voice is like music to my ears, a song I've been waiting to hear.

"I'll go grab us all a drink," Parker says, and Addison follows him.

My focus hasn't left Charity. Her head hangs low, and her feet shuffle a little. As I open my mouth to say something, Elsie speaks. "Come on, Charity. Let's go dance up a storm."

"Oh, I'm not sure. I don't dance." She laughs. I hear the hint of nervousness in her tone. Her words are lost, though, because she's already being dragged away by Elsie and Paislee. Jimmy stalks off in a huff.

Jerking my thumb in his direction, I say, "What's up with him?"

All the guys shrug. "That's who he is. Always angry, it seems," Dane says.

"Yeah, okay. Well, enjoy your night, and I'm sure I'll catch up with you all later." As I walk off, my eyes zero in on the makeshift dance floor where I stop dead, seeing Charity laughing while swaying her body from side to side. The way her hips move casts me under a captivating spell. My hands itch to rest on them and move with her.

I'm not a dancer, and I refuse to get out there with the other girls, no matter how much they beg. For her, though? I'd do it just to feel her warmth pressed against me.

CHAPTER
Nine

Charity

My goodness, I feel like a fool. This atmosphere isn't something I'm used to. There are so many people here, and the beats vibrate through me from my head to my toes. I've never been allowed to have music like this on. Especially not this loud.

"Move your body, girl. You have eyes on you." Paislee gives me a sly look. When I turn to see who she's referring to, heat rises in my face. Jase stands there, leaning against the doorframe. Damn, why is he so attractive? He seems to be everywhere I am lately.

"Ah, you're supposed to keep moving, not stop entirely." She takes my hands and starts moving them for me. I attempt to ignore the eyes that bore into my back.

It's not long before Parker and Addison arrive with some plastic cups filled with I-don't-know-what. My attention goes to Jase. His stare is heated, and without thinking, I lift the cup to my lips and swallow a mouthful. My face screws up. "This is disgusting," I say. The girls laugh.

"You never had a beer before?" Elsie asks as she throws back her own.

"Nope, never. I was always on a tight leash, you could say." I take another drink—slowly this time. The taste isn't so bad. Warmth spreads from my belly through the rest of me.

"Girl, you're about to live an entirely different life," Paislee says, bumping my shoulder. "Though we won't start with the strong drinks just yet." She laughs.

Suddenly, loud, rowdy voices pull us from our conversation. All heads turn to the doorway. Jase has disappeared. Dane, Parker, and Aiden take off toward the sound. We all follow, our interest piqued.

"We're not here to cause trouble. We just want to enjoy the night. We heard you guys put on some great parties; we wanted to come." The guy standing in front of Jase is the same height as him and almost equally as built. His dark hair and chiseled jaw would be enough to have him winning all the girls. A few men stand behind him.

I can't see Jase's face to have any idea what's going through his head. Judging by the commotion, I'd guess they're not a group people from the college like much. Leaning over to Addison, I ask, "Who are they?"

"They're the rival team. Obviously, they're here to cause trouble. I have no doubt about that. The guy standing in front of Jase is Alex, bigwig quarterback for RVU, also known as River View University. We call them the River Rats." She giggles.

"Oh, okay. He's cute." I smile.

"Yeah, he's cute, but he's their campus bad boy. He and Jase have been rivals since the beginning of their football careers. I'm betting Jase lets them stay, because that's the kind of guy he is, but he'll be sour all night because they're here." She pauses and gives me a stern look. "Now remember, they may be hot as sin, but don't get cozy. I've heard stories from other girls."

"Yeah, okay. I'll be sure to keep my distance." As I say it, it's as though Alex heard me. His eyes turn on me, and I can see it—lust fires in his eyes. *Damn, he is good.* My knees even go weak. *He's bad news.*

Addison is right; Jase lets them stay. The crowd disperses, and everyone goes back to what they were doing. Leaving the girls, I go in search of another drink. I've been monitoring how many I've had, and thankfully, they haven't gone to my head yet. Although, I have become a little chatty and grown out of my shell a bit.

Turning to enter the kitchen, I almost bump into Alex. I stumble back.

He reaches out and takes my arms to steady me. "Whoa, easy. You good?"

Pulling my arms from his grip, I say, "Yeah, thanks. Sorry. This place is crazy full, and I didn't see you until it was too late."

"Hey, that's okay. I'm glad it was you who ran into me." He winks.

"Oh, really? You don't even know who I am. I could be your worst nightmare for all you know."

He lifts an eyebrow. He leans into me; our faces are mere inches apart. My breath hitches at his closeness. "Oh, I hope you are. We could have some fun."

Pushing against his chest to put some space between us, I laugh. "You don't know me at all, and you've got me all wrong, buddy. I'm not *that* kind of girl."

Alex reaches up and runs his fingers down my cheek. I shudder at his touch. "What's your name?"

Before I can open my mouth to respond, a large frame steps up beside me. Jase stands there with his stony gaze right on Alex. I sigh. "Alex, can I help you?" he asks.

Alex steps out of my space and stands tall. "Nah, J. I was getting acquainted with this beautiful girl, and you butted in before I could find out her name." A grin tugs at the corner of his mouth.

Jase's arm wraps around my shoulders, and he pulls me against him. "She's not interested."

My head whips in his direction. As much as I want to stop this pissing contest, I don't have what it takes to ward off people like Alex. He's a smooth talker. I, for one, would have no problem hitting him where it hurts if he tried something.

Alex raises his hands. "All right. Sorry. Didn't mean to start anything." He moves around us, giving me a wink. When he disappears, my body instantly relaxes. I didn't realize I was so wound up and tense.

Jase's frame moves right in front of me. "Are you okay?" His worried electric-blue eyes bore into mine. My bottom lip trembles. This is the kind of scene I'm not accustomed to.

Stepping back, I straighten my back. "I'm fine, thanks," I snap, annoyed. "As much as I'm thankful to you for stepping in, just stop. I can handle things myself. I don't need a superhero today; I needed one for the last ten years." The last sentence is a slip in my façade. My hands tremble, and an ache forms right in the middle of my heart.

"Hey, whoa, I was looking out for you. Sorry for caring." He turns and stalks away.

Guilt rushes through every part of me. I chase after him. Grabbing his arm, I say, "Jase, stop."

He does; he doesn't look happy about it, though. His lips form a thin line. "What?"

I meet his heavy gaze. "I'm sorry. I didn't mean to bite your head off. I have a few things I need to let go of when it comes to you and me," I say, shocked at my blunt honesty.

His brow furrows, and he crosses his large arms over his chest. His tattoos catch my attention. "What things? Let's hash them out now so I can stop feeling as if I'm walking on eggshells around you. I've gone out of my way to try and fix whatever issue you seem to have with me."

"I know. I'm sorry. The issues are mine. I can't help the way I feel at the moment."

There's a beat of silence between us. Loud music thumps, and louder voices surround us.

"Perhaps it's better if I give you the space you need to sort out whatever it is you have going on." His words sting.

"Oh, okay. Well, if that's what you want." I stumble over my words, feeling foolish.

"I can't do this with you. This back and forth. I thought we'd agreed to be friends, yet you're still cold toward me. You can hardly make eye contact with me for longer than five seconds. What the hell did I ever do to cause you to hate me?" His arms tense as he speaks.

Swallowing the fear clawing in my throat, I say, "You forgot me, ignored me, and now you expect all to be forgiven. You don't know what my life has been like for the past ten years. You stand in front of me with everything you want at your fingertips. Screw you, Jase. Just pretend I don't exist. You're good at that." Before he can say anything else, I turn and storm off without the drink I was hoping to get.

Without watching where I am going, I numbly make my way outside when gentle hands grab my arm. "Sorry. My fault," I say as an automatic response.

"Hey, what's wrong?"

Relief washes through me. Paislee stands there. She takes one look at my face and drags me outside where it's a lot quieter. We pass Jase leaning against a wall, a drink in hand. His eyes follow me as I walk past him, boring right into mine. They're a little darker than usual, and there's something unreadable about him. Brooding. Desire throbs through me. *Stop betraying me, body.*

Paislee stops in a private place in the backyard. "What is going on? Did something happen?"

"No. It's me. It's all me. I'm so messed up, Paislee." Tears fill my eyes, and wetness dampens my cheeks. Quickly, I swipe the tears away.

"It's not you. Trust me."

"No, it is. I'm messed up."

Paislee pulls me into her arms, and the tears that leave me are like a flow of all that I've suffered over the past ten years.

CHAPTER
Ten

Jase

Paislee has her arms around a trembling Charity, and it's all my fault.

Charity's right. I don't know what she's gone through. I want to be a person for her to open up to, but when she keeps shoving the fact that I forgot about her in my face, I have no idea what the hell she means. I never forgot her, and the day she showed up here, my first thought was that I was dreaming. Perhaps I still am.

"What are you hiding in the shadows for?" I whip my head toward the voice. Addison comes and stands beside me. Her gaze follows where mine was. "Oh, I see."

Rubbing my forehead, I ask, "What?"

"I didn't say anything." She sounds shocked.

I give her a stare. "You don't need to. Your tone said it all."

She laughs. "Sorry. What's the deal with you and Charity? I caught your little exchange inside."

"There's no deal. We were friends before she left. We lost contact, and now she's back," I say, shrugging as though it means nothing to me, when really, it—*she*—means more to me than anything.

"What did you do to upset her? Hell, even I can see she's shaking from here." Her tone is harsh and accusing.

I raise my hands. "Stop right there. I did nothing. She keeps throwing things in my face that I know nothing about, and it's as though she's angry at me. For what? I have no idea. I just want to be her friend. That's it." I sigh.

Addison looks between me and Charity. "I think you need to go over there and check on her. The look in your eyes tells me you care deeply for her. Go be the bigger man." She has a point.

I push off the wall and make my way over to Paislee and Charity. Their voices are low.

"Hey, Charity?"

She turns at the sound of my words. When her face shifts into the light, I realize I'm such a dick. Her red-rimmed eyes speak volumes. Her makeup is streaked down her face. I'm an idiot.

"What?" she snaps while wiping her fingers under her red and puffy eyes to clear away her tears that still sit on her cheeks.

I glance toward Paislee. "Can you give us a minute?"

She nods and steps away but still stays close enough, probably to see if I cause her any more upset, and then she'll step in.

"Sorry about what I said. I'm just confused—that's all. The other day when I saw you at the park, I meant what I said. I want us to be friends again. If you can forgive my stupidity." Her eyes don't move from mine. The way she stares haunts me. If she wasn't so upset, I probably would kiss her. What would she taste like? Something sweet?

"I can't." She pushes past me and runs toward the door. She's gone in a flash.

"What is up with you?" Paislee has the same tone as Addison did.

"Nothing. She's the one with the problem. You better go after her; I tend to make things worse when it comes to her."

Paislee shakes her head and takes off as fast as she can.

What did I do wrong?

CHAPTER
Eleven

Charity

A light tap on my bedroom door wakes me. "Yeah?" I call.

"Hey, honey. How was your night?" Mom comes in and takes a seat on the edge of my bed.

"It was fine. What time is it?" I ask, rubbing my eyes.

"It's lunchtime. I was beginning to get a little worried because, since you've been here, you've been up early every day."

"I guess everything has finally caught up with me." I yawn, and my arms stretch over my head, then my entire body follows suit, followed by a long yawn. Can't say I've had a decent sleep like that in ages.

"Yeah, I thought that might be the case. I was going to see if you wanted to go shopping today and maybe get some paint for the walls and new curtains. Bring this room up to a better standard." She laughs while looking around. I follow her gaze. The pink is seriously outdated. The white dresser is covered with some hair products and the small amount of makeup I own.

"I'd like that. I have my bed arriving at some stage; I'm just waiting to hear back from the lawyer. It's a solid wood one that Dad bought for me just last year. Is it okay if we get rid of this one?" I tap the mattress beneath me.

Mom laughs, nodding. "Sure. Whatever makes you comfortable. We'll get some lunch while we're out. Paul will watch the little ones. It can be a day for just us."

Grinning, I say, "I'd like that."

She nods and then exits my room, closing the door behind her.

Over the last couple of weeks, I've been distant. I suppose I'm still trying to find my feet without all of the rules Father pushed on me.

I desperately wanted to let things between Jase and I go. I thought I could get past everything, but for some stupid reason, my heart can't release the chains that have been tightly wound around it for the past ten years.

After running from the party and Jase last night, I caught an Uber home. Paislee is a great friend, and I'm super glad she's one person I have on my side at the moment. She's kinda like a ray of sunshine peeking through the darkness that clouds me sometimes.

My cell vibrates on the bedside table. Rolling over, I grab it and pause at the unfamiliar number and messages from Paislee.

Paislee: Hey, just wanted to check in and see how you are today. Want to hang out later?

Unknown: Hey, Paislee gave me your number. Something about a blind date. She's persistent, I'll give her that. Wouldn't take no for an answer. LOL

I smile at the message. He's right. She's very persistent. I've been here not even a month, and she's already trying to set me up with some random. It's probably good for me to meet some new people, although I'm not sure about the whole blind date thing. What if he's some crazy? Surely she wouldn't set me up with someone like that.

I type a quick reply to her and the mystery man.

Charity: Please tell me the guy you're attempting to set me up with isn't a crazy madman. He just messaged me, and I'm not sure I'm ready. What if he saw my breakdown last night at the party? I would look like a complete fool. Also, I can't catch up today; I'm spending some time with my mom.

Charity: Hi, Mystery Man—yep, that's my nickname for you. To be honest, I'm not sure about blind dates. Don't they all turn bad at some stage or another? Sorry. I'm an overthinker. Please don't think I'm crazy. I'm not—or maybe I am, just a little. LOL

After saving his name in my phone as Mystery Man, I toss the blankets back, pull myself upright, and make my way to my closet. I slide my legs into a pair of black jeans and grab a simple black tee from my drawer. Picking up my foundation, my cell pings. My heart skips a beat; it could possibly be Mystery Man again.

Racing to my phone, my lips curl up into a big grin. It's him. Perhaps it's too soon to be excited over a strange guy contacting me… but how can he be strange if Paislee knows and trusts him? I'm putting a lot of blind faith in her.

> **Mystery Man:** Nice name. I have you saved as Mystery Girl—great minds think alike. Maybe we can be a little crazy together. I'm happy to tell you who I am if it makes you feel a bit better.

> **Charity:** No, I'd rather keep the mystery for now. It's fun. Is there a timeframe on when the actual date actually has to happen by?

> **Mystery Man:** There doesn't have to be. Unless you'd rather meet sooner rather than later? I'm okay with whatever you'd like to do.

I stare at his text. What do I want?

> **Charity:** I'm honestly not sure what I want to do. I like the mystery. How about we chat and get to know each other over the week, and then we'll make a decision after that?

Look at me being in charge and making decisions. It's all new to me.

> **Mystery Man:** So long as you're happy, then I am as well. ;)

I can't help the cheesy grin spreading across my face.

> **Charity:** Yep. How about we play a game of 20 Questions? You ask something, and then I will. You're allowed to pass on questions, though.

I head out the door with my heart feeling a little lighter and grab my bag on the way out.

"Are you ready to go?" Mom asks as I hit the bottom step.

"Yeah." I smile excitedly about what my future holds.

Mom and I hit the hardware store for some paint and supplies. It's great spending time with her and getting to know her. The nervousness that we both had at the start seems to have slowly started disappearing.

While driving home, my eyes remain on the outside scenery. It's a silent drive, but I sense Mom's gaze on me. She shifts lanes, and again I feel the weight of her on-and-off stare. "What's wrong, Mom?"

"Oh sorry, honey. I just got caught up in the moment. I still can't believe you're here. We're so happy to have you here with us."

Glancing over, I smile. "Thanks. It's really been great. I've already made some great friends and reconnected with some old ones." Though, I can't say I've been happy about reconnecting with Jase. We seem to clash every time we see each other, and it's always my fault.

"I'm so glad you reconnected with Paislee. She really missed you when you left, as did Jase." The end of her sentence catches me off guard.

"What do you mean Jase? I'm sure he just forgot about me."

"No, he didn't. He came around daily to check on me and to see if I'd heard from you. He did that for a couple of months."

My chest constricts. Perhaps he did care. Of course the issue would be me. It always is.

"Hmm, okay. I always thought he'd forgotten about me." My reply is low.

"Charity, are you okay? I don't know what happened between you and your father while you were away. I want you to know I'm here for you. If you want to talk to a professional, I'd be happy to arrange that for you as well. I only want the best for you." Her voice hitches. She clears it away quickly.

"I'm not ready to talk about Dad with anyone." Pulling my bottom lip between my teeth, I bite down—hard. Talking about him brings back a rush of emotions I'm not ready to deal with. How do you tell your mother, or even a stranger, that your father abused you? Not only physically, but emotionally. The last ten years have been some of the hardest I've endured.

"Did he hurt you?" Reaching over, she takes my hand, and I let her. The warmth that spreads through me from her touch is something I've missed.

Pulling my hand from hers, I rub my face with both hands. My eyes burn as tears well in them. "I really don't want to talk about it," I choke.

She's silent a moment then finally says, "It's okay. I'm here when you're ready."

I nod.

Will I ever be ready to talk about life with my father? No, I'd rather burn those memories from my brain, but I can't. There were days I wished someone would come and take me away from that house. Now I'm free. But how will I ever fit in when I still feel so tied to my past?

CHAPTER
Twelve

Charity

After dinner, I have a hug with Mom then make a quick exit. I think she got all she needed from our short conversation about Dad today. I collapse onto my bed when I hear my phone vibrate. I'd put it on silent when I went out with Mom and didn't really check it. I thought I'd get into trouble if I did. *Dad's rules.*

Dragging my emotionally exhausted body from the comfy mattress, I dig my phone from the bag I took shopping today. Five unread messages stare back. Smiling, I go head to my bed. I've never had a number of messages from friends. I shake my head to quickly erase the thoughts that were about to invade and stomp all over my happiness.

> **Paislee:** He's a good guy. So, when is the date happening? I'm so excited for you.
>
> **Charity:** No date set. I told him I wanted to get to know him before we did the whole date thing. Is that stupid?

This situation is a new one for me. I'm sure my question must have sounded stupid. While I wait for her reply, I read the other four messages from Mystery Man.

> **Mystery Man:** Okay, I can do that. So who goes first?
>
> **Mystery Man:** Since you've gone radio silent, I'll go first. What's your name? LOL
>
> **Mystery Man:** Don't answer that. I was being a wiseass.
>
> **Mystery Man:** Okay, serious question. What's something you enjoy doing?

My cheeks hurt from smiling so much. I type a quick reply.

> **Charity:** Gee, I disappear for a couple of hours, and you bombard me with messages. I'll admit, I kinda liked it. I felt important to someone. LOL. Now, as for something I enjoy doing... Hmm. If I'm being honest, I don't really know. I've been kept on a short leash for most of my life. Books have been my lifesaver. How about you? What do you enjoy doing?

My finger hovers over the send button. It's possible he'll read into the whole "short leash" thing. Maybe talking to this faceless stranger could be what I need. I never have to meet him if I don't want to—that's unless Paislee steps in.

Lying here, I can't help but think about the places my dad would take me to at the beginning. When we first moved, he took me to the local library, the park down the road, and shopping to get new clothes. Once we were alone in the big house, I suddenly became everything I never should have been at such a small age.

My cell pings, and I can't help the stupid grin that instantly pulls at my lips.

> **Mystery Man:** Should I be concerned? When you say kept on a short leash, how do you mean? As for me, I enjoy sports. In fact, it's my life. My father is a man who pushes what he wants onto his children, and so we're left picking up and doing the things he couldn't achieve himself. Sorry for my overload.

> **Charity:** Seems like fathers are a sore spot for both of us. I'm glad you have your sport, though. We all need something to make us happy. So tell me, what makes you happy, apart from sports?

Gee, I'm a little concerned at how fast he escalated and told me things about his dad. Perhaps his dad and mine were of the same mindset. I was never really given the chance to learn and grow and become me either.

Mystery Man seems to be taking forever to reply. My eyes become heavy, and I drift off into one of the most peaceful sleeps I've had in a long time. My thoughts turn to Mom and what she said about Jase. Perhaps I should give him another chance.

My alarm startles me awake. The vibrating right under my ear is not something I want to wake up to every morning. The weekend is nearly over, and today, Mom and I are starting work on my room. Opening my email, my eyes catch one from my father's lawyer. I release a sigh and then open it.

Good morning Charity,

I'm contacting you today to inform you that everything will be happening with your father's house this week. The movers are there to pack everything up. I've been informed that, unfortunately, I can't sell all the contents of the home as you had asked. So, we will be shipping everything to the address you provided. I'm sorry we couldn't do more. I've contacted a real estate agent on your behalf, and she will be in contact with you over the coming week.

If you have any questions, please feel free to give me a call, and I'll help any way I can.

Kind regards,

Marcus
Jacob & Son Law Firm

"Perfect. Now what am I supposed to do with all his junk?" I groan. How am I going to tell Mom that I have everything being shipped here? I doubt she and Paul will be happy about it.

Needing to clear my head, I pull on my tights, tee, and runners. Outside my window, it's still somewhat dark, the kiss of the sun only just starting to hit the tops of the high trees. The house even sounds quiet. After grabbing my phone and sticking it in the pocket of my tights, I quietly head downstairs and out the door.

As soon as I step out of the front gate, my feet hit the pavement with such a pace I'm not sure my lungs will be able to keep up. My world felt like it was slowly climbing on top of me and that soon I wouldn't be able to hold myself upright. Maybe Mom is right and I do need to talk to someone.

I stop at the same park I took Beau to the other day and collapse on the same bench, my chest tight and struggling to fill with air. I'm so not a runner. Pulling my cell from my pocket, I shoot a message to Mystery Man, ignoring the message he'd sent last night. He's the only person who doesn't know the true me.

> **Charity:** Why is life so hard? Why does it feel like everything is about to collapse all over me and I have no way of climbing out? I've been on my own for so long, and now I have to figure out life when it was previously run for me. What am I going to do?

Before I even register what I've written, I hit send and pull my legs up to my chest and place my forehead on my knees. I can't stop the tears that overflow. Sobs wrack my throat and tear my heart apart piece by piece as every part of me becomes numb.

"Charity?"

I glance up as a sob gets caught in my throat.

Jase stands there, a face of concern staring back at me. "Whoa, what's wrong?" He sits down beside me, and I cry harder.

"I can't make it stop," I wail. "How do I make it stop?"

Large arms wrap around me, and with such ease, Jase pulls me onto his lap, securing me against his chest. I don't fight it. I need him. Resting my head against his firm chest, I hiccup. My hands cover my face, and I concentrate on my breathing. In and out. *You're not allowed to cry and show weakness. Weakness is for the weak.*

Dad's words shock me to the core. It's as though he's standing beside me, whispering them in my ears.

But Jase's voice is much, much stronger. "It's okay, Charity. I've got you."

Jase does have me. I inhale a deep breath. His musky scent is intoxicating yet calming. As I concentrate on it, slowly the sobs that wrack my chest subside. "You're okay. I'm here." Jase's comforting words pull me further and further from the darkness that was slowly crawling into my heart and taking over.

Finally, it stops, and all I hear is Jase's breathing. Pulling my hands from my face, I lean out from his chest and stare at him. His blue eyes shine with unshed tears. "I'm sorry," I croak.

"It's okay. I'm just glad I could be here for you. What's going on? Talk to me. Please," he begs.

Swallowing, I say, "I'm not sure what to say or how to put it into words. Everything with my father is consuming me." A lump forms in my throat as I think about the pain I went through under his roof.

"In what way? Did he hurt you?"

I can't bring myself to say it, so I nod.

Jase's arms tense around me. "I want to help you get through this."

"I'm not sure you can. There's so much emotional damage done. I'm damaged goods. Not good for anyone."

"Don't say things like that," he growls. "You're so much more than you see."

Silence hangs in the air between us. I turn to him and steel myself for the bravest confession I've ever had to make. "I know this is a bad thing to say, but I'm glad he's dead."

CHAPTER
Thirteen

Jase

A nger slices through me, and I have an urge to hit and
hurt something or someone. Red blinds my vision as
everything she's saying sinks in. If that man who claimed
to be her father was still alive, I'd probably end up in jail
from killing him myself.

"It's not a bad thing to say. A part of me wants to go and
kill him all over again. Charity, I'm so sorry you went
through the things you did." I want to know details, but I'm
not sure she's ready to share them yet.

"I deserved everything. Well, that's what he said." She
shrugs.

"No, don't say that. You deserved *nothing*. If anything, you deserved to be here with your mom and surrounded by people who care about you."

Her eyes fill with tears. "You care about me?" She sounds shocked.

"You have no idea, Charity. And so does your mom. Please stop listening to the things your father put into your head. They're not true. Not one of them."

Her mouth opens slightly. Without thinking, I lean in and gently brush my lips over hers. They're cold and soft. She sucks in a breath. My hand comes up and holds the back of her neck, and I rest my forehead against hers. Our breaths come slightly quicker. I pull her tighter against me. Her body relaxes against mine.

We stay like this for what seems like a while. The desire to kiss her again is so overwhelming. She pulls back. Her eyes, shining emerald green and wide, stare into mine. The pull is so strong that, this time, I give in and press my mouth to hers again—only, hard this time. She responds by driving her hand through my hair and holding my mouth to hers. Our tongues clash, and our breaths become wild.

Never did I think I'd see her again, let alone be making out with Charity on the park bench. It's as though all my dreams have come true at once.

Out of nowhere, Charity rears back, her hand coming to her perfectly kissed lips. Her eyes have turned panicked.

"What's wrong? I'm sorry, I shouldn't have," I say.

Charity climbs from my lap and stands in front of me, rubbing her hands over her tights. I stand and take a step closer. She holds up her hand to stop me. I pause, then she says, "I… ah…" She fumbles over her words as her face drops into her hands, and she rubs it furiously. "What am I doing?" Her voice is barely a whisper, but I still catch it.

My focus doesn't leave her. I want to comfort her, help her though whatever it is she's struggling with. She pulls her phone from her pocket, and as the screen lights up, the name on top of an unread text catches my attention. *Mystery Man*. She's the girl I started messaging last night.

She's my Mystery Girl. Now her comment about her father makes sense. Her being kept on a short leash and how he obviously treated her.

"Charity," I start. She should probably know that it's me she's messaging.

"I can't do this." Without giving me the chance to explain, she turns and runs back in the direction of her home. I should go after her, but she obviously wants to be alone. Maybe Mystery Man might not be such a bad thing. I could possibly be someone for her to talk to. Will she be angry when she finds out it's me? It's a high possibility, but I want to be here for her.

Reading her message before, I thought for sure this girl I was texting was in serious trouble. Her tone in the text threw me. Coming upon Charity was a complete fluke. I'm so glad I could be here for her at this moment, even if I did screw it up by kissing her. Stupid move. Praying on her fragile state of mind is not something I'd normally do. But with the way she looked at me and how her plump lips stood out, I couldn't help myself.

Grabbing my phone from my pocket, I shoot her a quick follow-up message.

> **Jase:** Hey, I need to know you're okay. Your earlier message kind of freaked me out. Do you want me to call you?

Collapsing back onto the bench, I sigh. What has she gone through? That man has destroyed her confidence.

Fathers are supposed to care and give their kids opportunities. Speaking of fathers, at least mine has given me chances at big things. Of course, he's gone about it all the wrong way. The way he pushes and pushes has filled me with so much anger and annoyance toward him that I hate dealing with him. Charity's father obviously abused her, and now it's possible she's suffering without letting go of the things he instilled in her.

Minutes later, my cell vibrates.

> **Mystery Girl:** I'm fine. Sorry, I had a momentary freak out and became overwhelmed with everything going on.

> **Jase:** I understand. I'm here if you need a friend.

> **Charity:** I'm not sure. I'm not good at opening up about certain things. It's always just been me having to deal with what I've gone through and am still going through.

> **Jase:** I want you to know there's no judgment here. You need a person. Someone you can talk to without feeling worried or judged. You won't get either of those things with me.

> **Charity:** Thank you. I really appreciate it. Sometimes strangers make comforting friends. At least I know you aren't some crazy. LOL My friend who told me about you said you're a decent one. One of the good guys.

Mental note: Thank Paislee.

> **Jase:** She knows me well. I've got you. I'm here anytime you need a friend. Always.

CHAPTER
Fourteen

Charity

"Hey, Charity, are you coming tonight?" Paislee steps in beside me. It's been almost a week since my meltdown and kiss with Jase. As good as it felt, it also felt so very wrong. I shouldn't have allowed it to happen the second time; he tasted every bit as sweet as he is in person. I'm so glad he turned up, though. Who knows how I would have gotten through the breakdown without him?

Turning toward Paislee, I say, "I'm not sure."

I don't want to face Jase. Him witnessing my breakdown was embarrassing enough. Mystery Man has been fantastic, though. Always checking up on me and bringing a smile to my face daily. My phone vibrates. Pulling it from my jeans pocket, I can't help the grin.

> **Mystery Man:** Hope you're having a good day.
> Don't forget to smile and have fun.

It's his regular daily text. Something positive to bring brightness to my day.

"Who's that?" Paislee peers over and tries to see. I pull it away from her line of sight.

"It's the guy you're trying to set me up with."

"Really? And how's that going for you both?" she asks. The wicked grin on her face tells me she's pleased with her matchmaking skills.

"Good. He's been a great friend. I'm not sure I ever want to meet him. It might ruin everything," I laugh.

"I doubt that," she responds almost suspiciously. I'm about to ask her for more information on her cryptic expression when a rumble of laughter fills my ears and causes goosebumps to prickle over my skin.

"Hey, Jase," Paislee greets the wall of muscles standing in front of us.

"Hey, Pais," he says then turns his focus to me. "Hey, Charity. What are you girls up to? Are you coming to the game tonight?" His eyes shine when he asks. This game obviously means something to him.

"Of course! We wouldn't miss you guys smashing Alex's team, would we, Charity?" Paislee shoves my arm.

"Oh yeah, for sure." I stumble over my words, not sounding too convincing. It wasn't on my agenda to go anywhere tonight, but hey, it's got to be better than sitting around at home doing nothing except drowning myself in thoughts of bad memories.

The kiss with Jase has been on replay in my mind lately. He tasted like fresh mint, and the way his lips moved with mine? It was like they had been waiting their entire life for the electricity that happened inside of me the moment our lips touched. It was so real and so perfect.

A shiver runs down my back. My head whips up and meets Jase's soft, humorous stare. "I have no doubt it'll be a great game. Cheer loud for us." He winks then steps around us. A small part of me wanted him to talk to me more. I guess now isn't the time to bring up the kiss and my mental breakdown. When will be the right time, though?

"I guess you'll be at the game now." Paislee shoves my shoulder playfully against hers while laughing.

Rolling my eyes, I say, "Shut up. I was kind of put on the spot there."

"Do you like him?" She jerks a thumb behind her shoulder. Spinning around, I catch the back of Jase as he turns into a classroom. His head comes up, and our eyes connect and hold briefly.

"You mean Jase?"

She nods. "No, Mr. McKenzie. Of course I mean Jase, silly."

Her question surprises me, and I have no clue how to answer. Do I like him? He's attractive and has a caring side to him. "Um… I don't look at him like that. If anything, I hardly know him now. It seems we clash more than we actually get along at the moment." I laugh.

"Why is that?"

Shrugging, I say, "I think maybe I feel a little abandoned by him. We were so close when we were younger. If I wasn't hanging out with you, I'd be with him. In my young mind, he was the boy I was going to marry when I got older." A warm sensation spreads through me. "Gee, I must sound like a fool."

Paislee stops. "You're not a fool. If anything, I think the years you haven't been here have been some of your hardest. You're different from what I remember. You used to laugh so much more. These days, it's even hard for you to crack a smile. I get the whole 'feeling abandoned' thing. Maybe you should talk to him about it?"

I shake my head. "No, I can't sit here and blame him, even if I wanted to. Really, I'd just like to have a decent conversation with him without it turning into a fight because of me lashing out. He's done nothing but try to be nice, and I've been a bitch." I shrug, chewing on my lip.

Paislee starts walking again. "Well, I'm sure things will work out with you and him, even as friends. Let's go have a good night and forget about guys."

"Yeah, sure. Like hell you'll forget about guys. Your man is delicious." I wave my hands at my face as though I feel hot. We giggle and head to our next class.

Jase in regular clothes is a sight for sore eyes, but him in his football uniform has me wanting to pounce and ravish him. The way those tights hug each muscle of his legs is something else, and his body—it's already huge, but add in his gear, and his size doubles. Watching him run down people from the opposite team has me cringing, but it's such a rush. I can only imagine what it would feel like for him. He has such talent. His movements are fluid and…well…damn.

"Oh my goodness, did you see Jase smash Alex? I'm sure he'd snap me in half with a drive like that." Paislee flinches beside me.

"I now know why I've never really been into watching sports. It looks like it would hurt too much, and I cover my face every time something looks like it's going to cause broken bones or draw blood." I cringe.

Elsie cheers on the other side of me. This girl has got a set of lungs on her. I might be deaf in the ear closest to her after this game.

Cheering for our team to win has been some thrill. I've never been to a game, and the girls have had to explain things to me. Well, Paislee has; Elsie is pretty hopeless. She does know when we score, and when we hurt the opposite team, she screams her excitement.

"Look at Jase. Isn't he delicious in his uniform?" Paislee says as though she read my mind from a second ago.

"Yep, I have to agree with you there," I say. Elsie and Addison murmur their agreement. Their guys are away for a basketball game, and since Jase invited Paislee to come to the game, we made a thing out of it. I wasn't keen at the start, but now that I'm here, it's such an alive atmosphere—one I want to be involved in more. It makes the weight that's resting on my heart a little lighter.

Glancing down at the field where the players sit, my focus lands on Jase, who is now down on a knee in front of his coach who is talking with them all. He has his helmet off, and the second his eyes land on mine, my heart skips a beat. He grins and gives a small nod. It's as though a swarm of butterflies has taken up residence in my stomach. I can't take my eyes from him. His messy blond hair makes him look even sexier.

"Are you making eyes with Jase?" Elsie bumps me, pulling me from the staring contest I seem to be having with Jase.

Shaking my head slightly, I say, "No," but the flush that warms my face probably tells her all she needs to know.

Elsie laughs. "Oh. My. You *do* like him."

"What? No." My head flicks between her and Paislee on either side of me. Addison leans out and gives me a look that says *Don't lie*.

Oh, hell. How did I get myself into this mess? Well, not mess, per se, but I can't say outright that I'm head over heels for Jase. The sensation swarming in my stomach tells me something I never expected, though. Something I'm not ready to admit, even to myself, let alone the girls.

"Yeah, sure." Elsie smirks but doesn't push it anymore.

After the game, we stand around, waiting for Jase to come out. Paislee mentioned that she's organized for us to grab a bite to eat with him and Blane. Parker, Dane, and Aiden are going to meet us at the place.

It's crazy to think that I've only been here a short while, yet I feel like I belong. These girls make everything a hundred times better. I've never had friends like them, and now that I've finally found some people who accept me for me and have welcomed me into their group, I know I made the right choice in coming to stay here with Mom. But I needed someone. I had no one. One day, I'll tell Mom about Dad and what he was like. It's just too hard to talk about now as it's still raw.

Laughter catches my attention. I turn in that direction. Jase comes strutting out, his arm draped over another girl's shoulders. The happiness swarming in my stomach turns sour. The green monster has taken up residence on my shoulder. There's no reason for me to be jealous. He's nothing to me, and I'm nothing to him. The kiss meant nothing.

"Oh, there he is," Paislee says excitedly. "Oh, and he's got *her*." Her lips purse.

"Who is it?" I ask, confused over her reaction.

"A groupie. This one is from Alex's college. She's been trying to get Jase for, well, forever."

"Evening, ladies." All our heads turn toward the deep voice.

"Hey, Alex." Paislee smiles, but it doesn't touch her eyes.

His sights are set on me. A wave of unease washes over me. "What are you girls up to tonight? Want to come to a party at our place?" He throws his thumb over his shoulder toward the full cars of his team members.

"We're good, thanks. We already have plans," Addison says with a sweet smile. Now, she is one to watch out for. Her smile says she's sweet, but her eyes say *don't mess with me*. I like her.

Alex takes a step closer to me. I stiffen at his proximity. My back straightens, and I fold my arms over my chest. I take a small step away. "How about you? You look like you could have some fun." He grins, but it makes my stomach clench.

"Are you always this sleazy? Perhaps you should try taking the answer that's given instead of trying to force yourself on people who don't show an interest." I blurt the words out without thinking. Paislee laughs while Elsie and Addison start slow-clapping.

"Damn, girl. You tell him," Elsie says.

Alex takes a step back. His eyes actually soften. He raises his hands. "All good. Sorry to bother you. Thought maybe I could persuade you to come see for yourself that I'm not the bad guy people make me out to be." Surprisingly, he sounds genuine.

"Maybe another time when we don't have plans," I reply. The girls' eyes jump out of their heads. Their mouths hang open a little. The little green monster made me do it. Seeing Jase with the girl kind of flicked a switch.

"What do you want, Alex?" Jase practically growls.

Elsie chimes in before anyone else can speak. "Oh, Charity was telling him that perhaps next time we don't have plans, we'll go to their place for a party." I turn to face Jase. His face turns a shade of red. The girl he was with is nowhere in sight. Thank goodness for that. "Don't worry. She also put him in his place," Elsie adds a moment later.

"I think you should leave," he says to Alex. His hands clench at his sides as he takes a step and stands beside me, throwing his arm over my shoulders like he was doing not that long ago with a different girl.

"Yeah, okay. Catch ya, girls." Alex turns his back and walks away.

I pull myself out from under Jase's arm. "What is your problem?"

He opens his mouth to respond, then closes it, and then finally says, "What? I was helping."

"Pfft. I didn't need your help. You want to act all big and macho? You may as well piss on me and mark your territory. You're worse than a damn dog."

"Gee, where has this sass come from, girl?" Paislee asks with a nervous laugh.

"I'm just sick of feeling like a piece of meat being tossed to the dogs. Who kisses someone then never reaches out to them again?" I jab him in the chest. "You. You're not better than him." I nod my head in the direction Alex went. "Sorry, girls. I'm not going to dinner tonight. Suddenly, I'm not too hungry." I pivot on my heel to leave, but Paislee grabs my arm.

"Whoa, wait. He *kissed* you?" Her eyes widen as she turns her head between us.

"Yep. And then didn't say another word about it."

"Are you kidding me? You're better than that." She pokes him in the chest as I did seconds ago.

"Ow… come on. I didn't know how to approach you without you hating me more. I didn't know what was the right thing to do."

"Whatever," I say and storm off, not caring if the girls follow or not. I'm done with his macho man act. I don't need that drama in my life; mine is already like an episode of a drama-filled series.

CHAPTER ~~Fifteen~~

Jase

"What the hell just happened?" I say to no one in particular. Elsie and Addison run off after Charity. Paislee glowers, her eyes like daggers.

"You were an idiot—that's what just happened," Paislee snaps. "You're so much better than this. How about you try being the guy that I dated instead of this insensitive jerk?"

"Pais, I'm sorry. When it comes to Charity, something else takes over, and I become this overprotective idiot. It's not who I am."

"It's because you care, you fool." She shoves me in the arm then continues. "And you kissed her? Like, what the hell?"

She's right. I care more than I realized I did. "How am I going to fix this?"

Paislee's eyebrows pull down, and her stare is harsh. "Um, excuse me? How do you think you're going to fix this? You're not stupid. Well, you act stupid sometimes."

"I know what I did was the wrong thing. I shouldn't have been as protective as I was. But, Paislee, things for Charity weren't great with her dad. I caught her crying on the bench in the park the other morning. I comforted her and then kissed her. Wrong timing, I guess." I shrug.

She sighs. "Yeah, wrong timing. I know things weren't great for her. I've been trying to get her to open up to me, but she's locked up tight, and whenever anything about him is mentioned, she shuts down."

"She has been opening up in messages a little. I've been trying to talk to her more on a friend level and getting her to trust me as a person."

"Wait. You know it's her I was trying to set you up with?"

"Yeah." I explain to her how I saw my text on her phone after we'd kissed.

"Well, isn't this whole situation funny? You're messaging her, and yet, in person, you're not her favorite person. This is going to be interesting when everything comes out, and let me just say from past experience, it's better to be open and honest from the beginning. Secrets can get messy."

"I know. I'm not sure how to tell her, though. She's probably going to hate me no matter what happens. I can't do or say anything right by her at the moment."

"How about you stop acting like an overprotective boyfriend and just be her friend like you are in your text messages?"

"Yeah, I'll try to do better."

"No trying about it. Just pull your head out of your ass, and be the person I know you can be." She sighs then says, "I better go and catch up with the rest of them. Sorry about dinner."

I wave my hand. "Nah, it's me who should be saying sorry. I'll talk to you later."

Paislee turns and walks away, and I'm left standing here feeling very much like an idiot.

When it comes to Charity, it's like I become a different person to the one I normally am. Does that mean we aren't good together? What if we're not meant to be anything other than friends?

My phone vibrates in my pocket, and I dig it out. When I see it's Charity, a wicked grin pulls across my face.

> **Charity/Mystery Girl:** Can you explain something to me? Why are guys such dicks when you're not even with them and they have no right to act the way they are?

Here we go. At least I have a chance to explain myself. Paislee is right, though. I need to tell Charity it's me she's talking to. I type a quick reply.

> **Jase:** Wow, what a question. I think I need more information. How is said person acting? Are they being overprotective or just a dick in general?

> **Charity/Mystery Girl:** He's being overprotective. I appreciate that he's being like that, but I don't want to come across as someone who can't stand up for herself. Plus, me and this person have history, and I kind of need to let the past go. Maybe it's me that's the problem; that's usually the way it goes.

Her words cause my chest to constrict. It's not her, and I hate how she thinks it is.

> **Jase:** Whatever you do, don't ever think it's you, because most times it's never the case. Plus, I'm sure he cares about you. Guys have a funny way of showing they care. We're weird like that sometimes.

Gee, I sound like a philosopher. Heading to my car, I wait for her reply, which doesn't come. How can I show her that I do care about her?

The answer is clear.

I have to tell her the truth.

CHAPTER
Sixteen

Charity

Staring down at Mystery Guy's reply, I think he's probably right. Jase does care, otherwise he wouldn't have stuck around when I had my breakdown.

"So, what are we drinking to tonight?" Elsie squeals as she places a range of drinks on the table in the dorm living area where a pile of Chinese takeaway sits. I'm amazed it got here so fast. These girls sure know the places and people to get the things they want fast. I could learn a lot from them.

My hand wraps around a fruity-looking drink.

"How about to girl power?" Paislee says as she tips back a similar drink to mine.

"Sounds good to me. To girl power," I say, raising my bottle. The girls follow suit, and then we all take a mouthful.

The drink causes my tongue to tingle, and the taste is refreshing. I tip the bottle up and down another two large mouthfuls.

"Charity, you better eat something before you get too carried away." Paislee laughs and hands me one of the takeaway containers, which I accept and happily dig into.

A girls' night is something I've needed. Having all these new experiences has been great. I'm becoming the person I should be. No more being told what to do. No more rules. No more dresses. No more hurting. No more feeling worthless. I am so much more than what my father made me out to be. I wish he had left me with Mom, but then who would have been his regular slave around the house?

My stomach tightens at the memories of his fists connecting with my face and the time he broke my arm after twisting it too tightly. *He's dead.* I don't need to deal with him anymore. The thought of him has me taking more gulps of my drink, wishing to forget everything. He ruined me in ways I'm not sure I can overcome on my own.

"Yo, Charity, where did you go, girl? Did you hear what we were discussing?" Addison asks. She places some food in her mouth. All eyes are on me.

"Sorry, got caught up in my own thoughts. What were you talking about?"

Elsie says, "Paislee just told us it's your birthday next weekend."

Is it? I try my best to mask my face.

Elsie continues, "She suggested we have a joint party for the two of you at the guys' place."

"Yeah, I'm sure they won't mind at all. Between all of us, we can sweet-talk them." Paislee gives me a sly wink.

"Oh, it completely slipped my mind. I'm surprised you remember," I say.

"How could I forget? Our birthdays are a day apart. Did you forget?"

"It just slipped my mind, that's all. Sure, if you want to do something, we can. I'll have to check with Mom and see if she has anything planned." I can't believe I'd forgotten my own birthday. Yes, I write it on forms, but for me, over the past ten years, it's just been another day—nothing special. No presents, no party, and no love given from my father.

"That's okay. We'll have the party on Saturday night, which is my birthday, and because yours is Friday, you can have family time, given it's your first one being back with your mom, and I think she'll want to celebrate with you."

I suppose she would want to. "I'll talk to her tomorrow. We're decorating my old pink room at the moment. I can't believe she kept it the exact same as when I left."

Paislee takes a seat beside me. "Mom told me that your mom couldn't bring herself to clear your things out. She always had hope that you would want to see her again," she says. Her words are gentle, and I sense all eyes are on me. Keeping my head down, I aimlessly dig in the takeaway container, not wanting to meet anyone's gaze.

"Hey, you're okay. Don't go to a bad place." Paislee places a hand on my leg and squeezes. "Let's organize a party and have fun doing it."

"Yeah, okay." My words are soft.

"There totally needs to be lots of cake and plenty of drinks," Elsie chimes in, and they all talk amongst themselves, organizing the party.

Picking my phone up, I reply to Mystery Guy.

Charity: You might be right. Maybe how I feel about him has something to do with how I'm treating him. I have a lot of baggage that I don't discuss with anyone.

It's as though he's sitting on his phone, because his reply is quick.

Mystery Guy: Tell me three things about you that no one knows.

Damn. What kind of question is that?

Charity: That's a hard question. How about you go first?

Mystery Guy: 1. I'm jealous of my brother because he got away from the pushiness of our father. 2. I'm still harboring feelings for someone 3. I think she hates me. 4. My father rules my life, and everyone thinks it's great he shows an interest.

Charity: Wow. How do I top that? Okay, here goes nothing. 1. My father emotionally abused me. 2. I didn't even realize it was my birthday next Friday because my father never let me celebrate or acknowledge it. 3. I'm currently drinking alcohol for the second time in my life. And because you did four, so will I. 4. I understand the whole harboring feelings thing. I have a similar thing going on.

After hitting send, my heart doubles in beats per second. I literally told a stranger about my father. My mother doesn't even know; she has her suspicions, I'm sure, but nothing confirmed. My phone remains silent.

"Who are you talking with?" Elsie asks.

"Some guy Paislee is trying to set me up on a date with," I reply.

Elsie's head whips to Paislee. "Who is it? Do I know him?"

She shakes her head. "Nope, my lips are sealed. They'll find out when they go on their first date." She waggles her eyebrows before taking another sip of her drink.

"Personally, I don't want to know. I like not knowing," I say.

Paislee gives me a skeptical eye. "You really don't want to know who he is?"

I shake my head. "Nope. Not right now. When the time is right, all will be revealed." I laugh.

"Okay, so long as you're sure," she says.

"I am." I grab a different container of food and take a mouthful, followed by the rest of my drink.

"You should message your mom and let her know you'll stay here tonight," Paislee suggests.

"Oh yeah, I completely forgot. But I can walk home. It's not far away."

"You're not walking on your own," Addison snaps. "We can get someone to walk you back if you want to go home."

"Okay, I'll crash here. I'll send a quick message to Mom and let her know where I am."

Charity: Hey Mom, I'm going to stay with some friends tonight. Also, I realized it's my birthday this coming weekend, and Paislee and I are going to have a party on Saturday night. Is that okay with you? We can still do something on Friday night if you want. If you don't want to, that's fine as well.

Nerves wrack my body. I kinda feel like I shouldn't expect anything. As if I'm not worth it.

Mom's reply seems to settle some of the unease knotting in my stomach.

> **Mom:** Thanks for letting me know. As for your birthday, we can do something on Friday. Hopefully we can get your bedroom finished tomorrow so we can have everything set up and ready for when your bed and stuff arrives.
>
> **Charity:** Thanks, Mom. I'll be home in the morning so we can work on my room. Thanks for everything.
>
> **Mom:** Not a problem, sweetie. Have a good night.

The silence from Mystery Man is taking its toll. Maybe I shouldn't have said anything.

> **Charity:** Sorry if I said something wrong. This is why I keep things to myself. I don't want to scare people away from me.

Three sharp knocks at the door pull my attention from the message I just sent.

"It must be the boys. We should have told them to not bother," Addison says as she stands from the couch and opens it. There stand all their boyfriends and an extra. *Jase.*

CHAPTER
Seventeen

Charity

He's always got to show up. No matter where I go, he's there. I don't see this ending well. We've already had one argument tonight; perhaps we'll go for round two. We're like fire and ice at the moment. We aren't two peas in a pod—hell no. Yet, here he is, all swoonworthy-like and looking as hot as sin. Why does he have to look so tempting?

"Where's the party at, ladies?" Aiden's thick Australian accent carries through the door. "Look who we found downstairs. He looked like a lost puppy, so we put a leash on him and led him this way." Aiden chuckles as he claps Jase on the back then strides up to Elsie, planting a kiss on her lips. Her cheeks flush as he drops down beside her and takes the food from her and helps himself. They're super cute together.

"How did it go tonight?" Addison asks as Parker slips in beside her on the couch. I suddenly feel out of place. I'm beside Addison on the couch. Paislee and Dane are on the floor near the table, as are Elsie and Aiden. Jase kind of stands there, looking a little lost and unsure.

"Well, are you going to sit down, or are we going to turn you into the coat rack?" I ask teasingly. The room fills with laughter.

Jase smirks and shakes his head. Slowly, his large, familiar frame comes around and takes a seat on the ground near my leg. He leans against the couch, brushing his arm against my covered leg. Warmth spreads through me, and my mind buzzes.

"How was the game, Jase?" Parker asks as he picks up a box of food then settles back in beside Addison.

"Yeah, it was hard but good. We beat them."

"Nice. How was Alex on the field tonight?" Parker asks.

Jase's body tenses against my leg. Clearing his throat, he answers, "He's always full-on on the field. But it was an amicable game, and the refs were great as usual." He crosses his arms over his chest. His biceps bulge, and my fingers have a sudden itch to reach out and touch them just to know what they feel like. Having his arms wrapped around me like a security blanket is something I'll not forget in a hurry. If anything, I want them around me more. I give my head a little shake. *Stop thinking of Jase like that,* I grill myself.

"Weren't you girls supposed to go out to dinner with Jase tonight after the game? How did you end up back here and Jase downstairs?" Aiden asks, glancing between each of us.

I choke on the mouthful of soda I'd just taken a sip of. My chest heaves with coughs, and my eyes start to water. Only I'd make a fool of myself in front of everyone.

After a minute, I clear my throat. "Sorry, it went down the wrong way."

I look up as a glass of water is held in front of me. Jase hands it to me. Our fingers brush as I take it.

"Thanks," I say breathlessly.

"You good?" he asks, concern filling his eyes.

Nodding, I say, "Yeah thank you." I take a sip of the water to settle the urge to cough again.

Paislee offers the excuse to the boys. "Well, there was a little disturbance with Alex, and we got angry with Jase for the way he acted." She shrugs unapologetically, giving Jase a knowing glance.

"I lost my cool. That's all," he responds as he takes his seat again on the ground beside me. I place my hand on his shoulder and give it a light squeeze. He needs to know that I'm okay with it. More okay than I was in the heat of the moment. I need to stop acting like a brat. That's not me. I'm better than that.

His hand reaches up and rests over mine. Something unspoken between us is happening. My stomach twists as he squeezes my hand and then pulls away. The loss is an instant insecurity that floods inside me.

When my head comes up, I catch Paislee's eyes zeroed in on us. A brilliant white-teethed grin is on her face. She caught the exchange, and I still haven't moved my hand. I don't want to. Holding onto him is like gripping a pillar of strength. The past needs to be forgotten, and in this moment, it has been. He may have never reached out to me, but we were nine, and what nine-year-old keeps in contact? Probably none these days. They're all caught on technology.

"Well, Jase, you should probably learn that when you anger one of the lionesses, then the whole pack will turn on you." Parker chuckles.

"Damn straight," Elsie agrees.

"One hundred percent," Paislee says, shoving Dane in the shoulder. "We stick together."

"These girls are like the sisters I never had. Devon is great, but having this tribe as my sisters is even better." Addison's eyes shimmer with unshed tears. She quickly clears her throat and takes a sip of her drink.

My arms wrap around myself, and an ache in my chest slowly tears away at the brick walls around my heart. *What is happening?* I've never had this kind of connection with people. The girls are like a sisterhood I've not experienced before.

"Hey, are you alright?" Jase asks.

I nod. Is this what it feels like to have people care for you? To show love?

"Charity, can you help me with something in the bedroom? I need your help," Paislee says.

Without saying a word, I get up and follow her. The people behind me have become silent. I must be a defective person. Always causing problems. Is that why Dad did what he did? Why he was so hard on me?

The door clicks into place behind me. "What's going on? One minute you were fine, and the next it was like a switch flicked." Paislee's worried gaze holds mine.

"Am I the problem when it comes to Jase?"

Paislee pulls back at my question, her eyes curious. "What do you mean, the problem? You're not any kind of problem—not for any of us. We're your friends, Charity." Her voice is soft and calming.

"But tonight was all my fault. And when I hear you girls talk about how close you all are, I can't help but think that I'm the one with the problems. I told the guy you're trying to set me up with tonight that my father emotionally abused me. Then he simply shut down and didn't respond. I come with too much baggage. I'm broken, Paislee, and I don't know how to build up the strength that you girls have." Wetness coats my cheeks as I unload all my fears—well, not all, but some.

Without saying a word, Paislee pulls me into her arms and secures them around me. Hers aren't the arms that I want to be wrapped in right now. Eventually, she pulls back. "You are not the problem. You're an amazing person who has so much to offer those around her. I'm sorry you went through that with your father. If you ever want to talk, please reach out. I don't want you going through this alone. You aren't alone. And as for the guy, give him some credit." She bites her lip a moment before she blurts out, "Because he's sitting out there." She points to the door.

"Um… what? Jase?"

Her face scrunches up as she nods.

"He's the guy you were setting me up with?"

"Yes, and I'm sorry I didn't tell you. I should have. He didn't want me to tell you."

"Why?" A rush of excitement pours over me, and suddenly, I feel like a kid in a candy store.

"He wanted you to have someone you could talk to. Someone you could trust. Do you know what I mean?"

"Strangely enough, I do." The words come out slowly. Stepping out of her arms, I wrap mine around me again.

I meet her worried face. "What am I supposed to do now? Should I tell him that I know it's him? I've never been in a situation like this. And if I'm being honest, I've never even kissed a guy until Jase." Heat rises from my chest and settles on my cheeks. My lips turn up in a superstar grin.

Paislee laughs. "What if you don't say anything? He knows it's you messaging him. He saw a message on your screen at some stage. So, you now both know, but he doesn't know that you know it's him. This is crazy."

It's as though I've been shot by a rush of adrenaline. "Oh my goodness."

She shakes her head. 'This is going to get interesting now, isn't it? Don't shut him out, though. Let him be there for you. You like him, don't you?"

"I do. Though he probably thinks I hate him or that I'm a crazy person. I'm so hot and cold at the moment." I run my hands through my hair and take a breath. I can't believe this. I've been messaging Jase for the last week or so, and he knew it was me, and he's still talking to me in messages but not so much in person. I've been super high maintenance lately with all these stupid emotions ramming into me like fists into a punching bag.

She takes a grip on my shoulders. "Trust me when I say he doesn't think you're a crazy person. Personally, I think he cares deeply about you. He can be a stubborn male sometimes. All us girls in there have stubborn men." She laughs. "You know, you could use this to your advantage, if you know what I mean," she says slyly.

I shake my head. "I'm not sure that's a good idea. What if it all turns out bad? What if we keep fighting in person?"

"I doubt that. I saw you both out there just now. There is so much already between you, yet you're both as stubborn as each other. Just open your heart and let someone in. Trust me. You've got this. It's time to enjoy life, Charity. Allow him to show you a love that you haven't experienced,"

Paislee whispers, but her words ring loud and clear in my messed-up head.

It's time to let love in.

CHAPTER
Eighteen

Jase

What is going on in there? One minute she was fine, and the next everything about her changed. Perhaps these kinds of situations with everyone here might be too much for her. But when she told me what her father had done to her, I needed to see her and know she was okay.

After I'd read her message, anger had rushed through me like a bush fire with wind behind it. If that man were still alive, I probably would kill him myself. How could a father do that to his daughter? Is this why she's so defensive, always got her guard up? I have a desperate urge to take a sledgehammer to her walls and force her to let me in, but that's not going to work. Slow and steady will win the race with her.

Pulling my phone from my pocket, I send her a quick message while she's still in the room with Paislee.

> **Jase:** You could never say anything wrong. We may not know each other very well, but I want you to know I am here, no matter what. I'm so sorry you went through what you did with your father. I wish I could take that pain away from you. So, it's your birthday soon… Tell me one thing you wanted that you never got.

As I hit send, the bedroom door flies open, and laughter filters out.

"Hey, what did we miss?" Elsie asks. My focus stays on Charity. Her eyes shine as though she's been crying. What went on in there?

"Oh, nothing. I wanted her opinion on something." Paislee shrugs off Elsie's question, and Elsie doesn't push it, which is strange.

Charity pulls her phone from her jeans pocket and smiles down at it. The weight sitting on my chest lifts slightly. Still doesn't help the anger I feel toward the man who hurt her.

Her fingers glide over her phone, and then she comes and sits down in her seat, and again, her leg brushes my arm. My phone vibrates in my hand, alerting me to another message. Thankfully, I'd thought to put it on silent before I came in the dorm.

The way she makes me feel is nothing like I've experienced with girls in the past. She's different. She's special. Warmth hits my shoulder, and I realize it's her hand again. Tingles spread from my chest and down my body. Again, I reach up and take her hand. This time, I don't take it away. I want her to know I care. I curl my fingers around hers to keep it in place. I can't help but wonder what she is thinking. What did her message say?

"Do you want another drink, Charity?" Elsie asks.

"Yeah, sure. Thanks." She sounds happier.

"So, everyone, Charity and I share a birthday weekend. We're hoping you guys will host the party of a lifetime next Saturday at your place." Paislee turns to her brother, Parker; she has puppy-dog eyes for him.

He's silent for a moment before answering. "Yeah, that will be fine. We have a game here next week." Even if he said no, I would have offered up my place. Charity needs a birthday party. She needs to experience what good friends do for each other.

Paislee claps excitedly. "Yay, planning time."

Hours later, it's after midnight, and we're all sitting around watching one of the Marvel movies. I think it's the last *Avengers*. I haven't been able to concentrate since Paislee moved to the ground beside me. She lies, stretched out, with her hands tucked under the pillow her head is resting on. Our hands are almost touching. Heat radiates between us; it's almost electric.

I stare at her. I wish I could take away all the pain she's experienced. Her hand shifts and is right beside mine. My fingers inch closer and closer. Swallowing the nervous lump in my throat, I glide my pinky against the side of her hand. This is the kind of move I'd put on girls when I was in high school. But Charity needs gentle and slow. I intend to deliver that.

Her finger moves against mine. Taking it as an invitation, I curl my hand over hers. A wave of exhilaration rushes over me. You'd think I'd never held hands with a girl before. Charity is different. She's the one who left, and I lost her. I'd thought she was gone forever, yet here she is beside me, gripping my hand as tightly as I am hers.

When the movie ends, all the guys leave, and the tired-looking girls make their way to their beds. Charity stands from the ground and stumbles back slightly. I reach out, take her arm, and steady her.

"Thanks, just a little light-headed. I got up too fast."

I keep my hold on her. She shifts a little closer. Moving my arm, I drape it over her shoulders. Thankfully, she doesn't fight me or move away.

"Charity, you can sleep in Willow's bed if that's good with you," Addison says. I swear, Willow and Jane are never here anymore.

"Yeah, that's fine. I'm going to bed. My body is screaming at me to sleep." As she says it, her body sways against mine.

"Here, I'll help you so you don't fall flat on your face. You're swaying right now." I chuckle. No one else says anything, so I lead her in the direction of the room.

She sits on the bed the minute she gets close enough to collapse on it. "Gosh, I don't think I've felt this tired ever." She rubs her face. Hesitantly, I take a seat beside her. She's so beautiful.

"Sorry about earlier and being all macho man. It's not who I am, but when it comes to you..." My words fade.

Charity's hand reaches out and takes mine. "It's okay. It's probably me. I tend to overthink things sometimes. Maybe this time we can actually start over."

My thumb glides over her knuckles. Her skin is smooth and soft. "I'd like that very much."

"Me too," she whispers.

"Charity..." My body wants her. My lips want to taste her, to caress every part of her in ways that make her forget her past. Swallowing, I ask the burning question that sits on the tip of my tongue. "Can I kiss you again?"

She sucks her bottom lip in between her teeth. Even that small move does things to me. The urge to jump her pounds in my chest, but I use every bit of strength in me to hold back until she gives me the all clear.

Her face meets mine. "I'd like that." My hand wraps around her neck, and I thread my fingers through her hair. I pull her against me. My heart thrums with anticipation. Our noses gently touch, her eyes close, and I memorize every freckle that splays across her nose and cheeks. She has captured me, and I'll gladly be her prisoner.

Gently, I press my mouth to hers. A small groan erupts from her throat, which causes my senses to go into overload, but I refrain from becoming a pushy asshole. Scaring her away isn't what I want. She's a fragile flower, and one wrong touch could crumple her. I won't be the one to cause her pain. Love is what I want her to feel when she's with me. I'll be her security if she'll let me.

Charity presses her lips harder to mine, and I don't let her pull back. Instead, she opens her mouth and allows my tongue access, and it soon becomes a tangle of tongues. Together, we're electrifying. I am the current, and she's the zap that follows. She's all I want.

With one swift move, she lifts her leg over my lap and straddles me. Our kiss deepens. Desire radiates between us. My hands slide down her back and over the curve of her hips, stopping on her perfectly shaped ass. As I slide her closer to me, a sigh rips through my chest.

"You're so beautiful, Charity," I say, pulling back a little so she can see the truth in my eyes.

"Do you want to know something I've never told anyone else?" she asks.

I nod.

"You're the first guy I've ever kissed." Her cheeks become a rose color, and her admission has me wanting her more. Now I know, without a shadow of doubt, that I have to take things slow with her.

"Thank you for sharing that with me. I hope you enjoyed it." I grin. My fingers trace down her jawline and along the bottom of her lips.

"I did." Her warm hands take the sides of my face and pull me toward her. Our lips collide again. This kiss is full of passion, love, and desire. She tastes like the candy we've been eating. So sweet.

Pulling back again, I reluctantly say, "I should go. You need some rest."

"Okay. I'll talk to you later." With one last chaste kiss, she climbs off me. My lips are left tingling and calling to hers with such a power I have to bite the corner of my mouth to stop myself from speaking.

As my hand lands on the door handle, I turn around. She sits on the edge of the bed, her hair slightly tousled, a sight that causes my heart to hammer.

"Screw it," I mumble before stalking back to her. Her smile is wide, as though she's won a prize. "One more. You tease me."

She laughs, falling back. I lean over her. My fingers trace up under her shirt and dance over her skin. She's a temptress with magical powers, and with one look, she's got me crazy for her even though I know I need to leave. I pepper kisses over her stomach, making my way up her neck and stopping on her mouth.

I sigh. "You captivate me, Charity. My temptress."

CHAPTER
Nineteen

Charity

This entire experience is a whole new world to me. Jase is tender and respectful, even though my body aches for his touch all over. He steals my breath every time his lips touch my sensitive flesh.

"Thank you," I say between heated kisses.

His head comes up. His eyes are questioning. "For what?"

"For being you and not giving up on me. I'm not the girl you remember. I've been through so much, and being able to share this moment with you is special." The words get caught in my throat, and the burn in my eyes becomes too strong. The tears pour out before I can contain them.

Jase is off me in a flash, pulling me into his lap. He rests his head against mine and lets me cry.

"I'm here." Two simple words speak volumes. He stands with me in his arms and then lays me down on the bed and slips in beside me. "If you want me to, I can leave, or I can go after you're asleep, or I can stay. The choice is yours." He presses a kiss to my forehead.

"Stay." It's him I want. His comfort, kindness, and support. Being in his large arms and pulled against his sturdy frame, I take a deep breath, locking to memory his familiar musky scent. It's calming and settles the bundle of emotions bursting through me as though fireworks have gone off inside me. Listening to his breathing lets the blanket of sleep come soon. Hopefully, my dreams are full of Jase and not the nightmares I've been enduring lately.

My body slowly wakes from a perfect sleep. A tattooed arm is draped over my waist, and hot breaths hit the back of my neck. My mouth pulls into a grin. Jase. I don't want to move. Lifting my arm, I take one look at my watch and freak out. Bolting upright, I startle Jase.

"What is it? What's wrong?" He rubs his eyes as I climb over his body.

"I'm late to meet Mom to get something to finish off my bedroom. I was supposed to meet her ten minutes ago. We'd planned this earlier in the week, and it just skipped my mind."

Jase stretches. I pause. His shirt rises a little, and there's a visible six- or possible eight-pack under there. "I can take it off if you want me to." He cocks a grin.

"Shut up. I've got to go," I say. Jase gets up and slips on his shoes, as I do mine, and we leave the room. Opening the door, we're greeted by the same group of people we spent time with last night.

"Damn, if I had known we could have slept over, I would have stayed," Aiden teases. Elsie backhands him in the chest.

"Shut up," she says through gritted teeth.

"It's okay. We only slept, and now I'm late meeting Mom." The words clamper out of me; I'll be surprised if they understood it.

"I'll drop you home. Come on," Jase offers.

Five minutes later, we pull up out the front of my place. A wave of nerves crashes over me. "Ah… thanks for last night." I can't help the flush that hits my face. He makes me feel stupid, but in a good way.

He leans across and places one small kiss on my lips, and it's as though my body lights up like a Christmas tree. It wants more. More kisses. More touches. "I'll talk to you later."

"Okay." Climbing out of the car, I'm left breathless. I watch him drive away. Last night, I really kissed him again, and we slept in the same bed. Oh my goodness, my father would be rolling over in his grave. A shiver stabs down my spine as his words punch me in the chest. *If you kiss a boy, you're a slut. If I find out you have ever done that, there will be hell to pay. You're a good girl, Charity. Good girls don't let boys kiss them or touch them. Rules are rules, and one is NO BOYS."*

Slut. Is that what I am? Surely not. My father was a liar. Of course I can't believe anything he told me. My stomach twists and knots. Anxiety creeps over me like a hundred ants on my skin. My breaths get short and thick, like I can't pull in enough air. Crouching down on the sidewalk, I'm sure I must look crazy to anyone looking.

"Charity? Are you okay?" Mom's panicked voice comes from our house. Within seconds, her arms are around me, pulling me up. "Come on, honey. Let's get you inside." She's such a caring person. Why did she let that man take me? She should have fought for me. I am her daughter as well. He told me she didn't want me.

Mom rushes me past Grace, Beau, and Paul, up the stairs and into my bedroom. She sits me down on the edge of the bed. "Charity, what's wrong?"

My eyes meet hers. "Why didn't you fight for me? Why did you let him take me?" Tears well again and cascade down my face.

"Oh, honey. It's nothing like that." Mom sits beside me and wraps me in her motherly arms. Sobs slam into me like tidal waves crashing against the shore. Mom lets me cry until I'm sure there's no more left in my tear ducts.

Mom leans back. "Charity, I love you. Why don't you tell me what happened? How can I help you?"

I want to be angry with her. I can't, though. "First, I want you to tell me what happened and how I ended up living with Dad instead of you."

She sighs. "I knew this was coming; I just didn't know when. Your father was an abusive man. Not only physically, but emotionally. He tore me down until I was a shadow of myself. I'd admitted myself to a hospital of sorts that helped me sort through everything he'd filled my head with. Charity, there came times where I didn't want to live anymore. You were my reason for living, but the more he ripped me to shreds, the more I felt worthless as your mother. I wasn't strong enough to fight him for you. So, while I was in this place, getting the help I needed, he packed his and your stuff and left. It was Jase that came over with your new address."

Pain claws at my chest as she speaks. "So he hurt you too?"

Her eyes fill with tears as she nods. "He did. Is that what he did to you?"

"Yes. I wasn't allowed friends, and if I did something wrong, he'd hurt me."

"Just know that whatever he told you is wrong. I came to take you back with me not long after you left, and he beat me too bad and said that you would receive the same treatment if I ever came back. I thought I was doing the right thing by you; I guess I was wrong. I should have done more, fought harder. Tell me what happened outside," she says, lifting one of her legs to rest on the bed. I do the same.

I rub my face. She's been through so much, and she let me go to try to save me. If only she knew the truth. "Jase kissed me last night," I say, my words low.

"Oh, honey, that's exciting."

I shake my head. "No, Dad always said if I kissed someone, it would make me a slut. That it'd make me dirty and that no one would ever want me. Please tell me he's wrong. I'm not a bad person, am I?"

Mom rests her hands on my shoulders. "Now you listen to me. That man was poison. He infected everything he touched and hurt those he was supposed to love and care for. You are beautiful and smart. Don't let his poison ruin your life like it did mine. I'm so sorry I left you there. So, so sorry." She yanks me against her chest, and we sit there, crying all the tears of lost years and so much hurt from one man. "Can you ever forgive me?"

I swallow the lump in my throat. "Yeah, of course. I just wanted an explanation. I'm sorry he hurt you as well. Looks like you've done so much better, though." I tip my head toward the door.

A smile brightens her eyes. "Paul's perfect, and I have no doubt you'll find someone to treat you the way he treats me someday too."

"Thanks, Mom."

"I'm here any time you want to talk. If you want to talk to a professional, I can organize that as well. You tell me what you need, and I'll sort it out."

"I think it will just take time," I say.

Mom kisses my forehead and says, "We don't have to do anything today if you don't want to."

"No, I want to do it. It's not much. Just the final touches before my stuff arrives. Oh, I forgot to mention that all the stuff is being shipped here. Is that okay?"

Mom smiles. "Of course. You can put it in the shed out the back and sort through it as you need to. I'll help if you want." She has such a great heart, and I'm so glad she's my mom. We've both gone to hell and back. She managed to climb all the way out and start fresh while I'm still clinging to the rock wall, hoping not to slip and fall down the rabbit hole of hell again.

"Thanks, Mom." I sniffle.

"You're my daughter, and I love you. I'd do anything for you." She pauses a moment then says, "Do you want to give today a miss? It's okay. We can do something else."

Shaking my head, I say, "No. I've been looking forward to it."

We spend the rest of the day laughing and enjoying each other's company. The uncertainty I had coming here is gone. Coming home was the best thing I could have done for my mental state. Being with Mom and my siblings has taught me that love is so much stronger than anything that my father showed me. He was a monster, and the best thing that happened to me was him dying—otherwise I'd still be there, living that life.

Poor, damaged Charity. That girl is still inside me, but I plan to push her so far into the back of my mind that she's nothing more than a distant memory. Sure, there are going to be times when I break. But I have amazing people to help pick up the pieces, and that's what matters.

CHAPTER Twenty

Jase

When I finally got the chance to read her message yesterday, it brought the biggest smile to my face, and it even made dealing with my dad a whole lot better. She'd said she wanted to meet *Mystery Man* as her present. Too bad she's already met him. With my dad on me and my brother coming home to give a talk at the college, I haven't had a chance to reply.

Now, here we are on Monday, and I've still not seen her around campus like I normally would. It's as though I have a Charity radar locked into me. When she's near, it's as though there's a current pulsating between us. We're drawn to each other.

"What's up, little brother?" Lachlan steps in beside me. We're very similar in height and build. I'm probably a little wider in the chest, but if that was ever brought up, he'd bring up that he's lightning on his feet. He's a great quarterback—a superstar, the news reporters say.

"Hey. How was Dad this morning? I had to get out of there before he gave me the *'Be like Lachlan'* speech." Rolling my eyes, I shove him with my shoulder.

"Trust me, once you get drafted somewhere, you'll be home free to make any decision you want—except if you make some dick moves and end up in the papers and on the sports channel for the *wrong* reason." He gives me a sideways glance. Lachlan is a popular and well-known ladies' man. He recently got into some hot water with some girl he slept with. She tried to fake a pregnancy. That wasn't happening on my father's watch.

"Yeah, man, that was a dick move. I hope you've reined in Little Lachlan now." I laugh, tipping my head toward his crotch.

He shoves me. "Shut up. It's not *little*. But yes, I've been told that if I don't pull my head in, I risk losing contracts for my future in sports. No one wants someone who draws negative attention to their team."

"That's good. Get your head in the game, brother. Not in women's pants." My stab results in another shove. My body slams against someone else. I hear a yelp in pain, and then the electric current rushes through me. I don't even need to look to know who I've been pushed into.

I whip around. Charity is on the floor, cradling an armful of books. "Oh, I'm so sorry. My dick of a brother did it." I pull her upright. Her shining eyes meet mine, and she winces slightly. "What's wrong?"

She shakes her head. "It's okay. Just landed on my hip. It'll be fine. How was your weekend?"

She's being a lot shyer than the last time I saw her. Just two days ago, she wanted to be close to me.

"It was the usual. Football, and my annoying father, and my brother came home. Speaking of, this is Lachlan. Lachlan, this is Charity."

He steps forward and takes her hand, giving it a shake. "Pleasure to meet you. Sorry for pushing big boy, here, into you. He can be clumsy sometimes." He laughs.

"It's okay. It's not the first time it's happened. Probably won't be the last, given my track record so far. How long are you in town for?" She seems genuinely interested.

"I have to head out today after I give this talk. You know, build up the spirits of young footballers and push them to pursue their dreams and all that. Hey, are you the Charity that Jase hung out with when he was a kid?" Lachlan points at her and gives her a questioning look. My stomach drops, unsure how she'll take this line of questioning.

Her nervous eyes dance between Lachlan and me before she says, "Yes, that's me," with confidence.

"Wow, you're back. That's awesome. It was good to see you again. Baby boy here was a smitten kitten when it came to you," he teases, clapping me on the back so hard that the air whooshes out of me.

Charity giggles and looks away. "Ah... so I've heard. Anyway, I better get going. I'll see you both around." She holds my gaze for a beat longer, and for the faintest second, her lips tug up on one side.

My eyes follow her as she walks away.

"Brother, can I give you some friendly advice?" Lachlan asks.

"Sure." We start heading in the direction of the hall where he's supposed to be talking.

"Don't let that girl go. I've only just met her for a second, but I can clearly see there's something between you two. The way she looks at you and you look at her—like I said, you're a smitten kitten. I had that once, but I was stupid. So damn stupid. I won't let you make the same mistake. So if she's someone special to you, don't let her go."

"I don't plan to," I reply. Now that I've got Charity in reach, there's no way I plan to let her go—that is, unless she wants me to. I won't force her to stay anywhere she doesn't want to or be with me just because it's what I want. She's so much more than a conquest. She's the queen, and I'm at her beck and call until the day she lets me in to become her king. I'll wait.

CHAPTER
Twenty One

Charity

Still nothing. Jase, aka Mystery Man, hasn't replied to my last message from Friday night, and now it's Monday and I've even seen him. Did I read the whole situation wrong? It's possible, given this is my first real interaction with a guy. Maybe I messed it up somehow.

Sitting here in class, not really hearing what the teacher is talking about, I stare at my phone as if willing it to light up with a message from him. *It's okay, Charity. He's been busy with family.*

Even as I think about it, I know I shouldn't feel like this. It's not like he's mine, and I'm not his. Well, not officially. He doesn't even know I know it's him messaging me.

I can't take the silence any longer. After unlocking my phone, I type a message.

Charity: Is everything okay? It's fine if you don't want to meet me. It was simply a thought that popped into my head. Perhaps we should just spill the beans on who we are.

I'm done with the game. I want him to know it's me. Damn, I wish I knew how he felt. Part of me thinks it's possible that he does like me and enjoys my company. After all, he did kiss me again. We made out and slept in the same bed together. Or is this something he does often? Kiss a girl and then hightail it and forget all about her?

Stop overthinking, Charity, I berate myself.

My phone vibrates, startling me so much that I jump in my seat.

Mystery Man: Sorry, the weekend got away from me. Things were a little crazy with the family. How was your weekend? Meeting you would be great. When did you want it to happen? I missed talking to you this weekend.

My heart rate speeds up. He missed talking with me. He missed me. I don't think I've ever been told something like that before.

Charity: My weekend was good. I had a good conversation with my mom after a slight breakdown. Things are better now. I won't say great, but better. We finished off my room, and now we're just waiting for some stuff of mine to arrive to add the finishing touches. We can meet whenever you want.

Mystery Man: Are you okay?

Charity: Yeah, I'm okay, or at least I will be. It'll be a process. So, apparently, I've got a party this weekend. How would you feel about meeting there?

Mystery Man: I'd like that very much. I have to run. I'll talk to you later.

Pop! There goes my happy balloon. Why can't he talk to me longer? I wonder what his reaction will be when I finally tell him I knew it was him.

"It's my birthday," I say to myself in the confines of my room as I lie in bed, staring up at the plain white ceiling. The birds are chirping outside, and I smile. *It's my birthday.*

My door flies open, and Gracie comes charging in and jumps up on my bed. "Happy birthday, big sister!" She sits on her knees, using them to bounce herself, causing my body to move with each bounce. "I made this for you." She hands me a sheet of paper with a drawing of two stick figures which I'm assuming are people.

"Wow, this is so cool. What is it?" It's probably the best present I've ever received. I don't remember my birthdays with Mom before I was taken away. There are small memories that pop into my head at times, but I wonder if they were even real.

She comes and lies beside me and points to one pink person—the bigger of the two. "This is you, and this is me."

"Oh, I love it. I'll have to add it to my wall. Thank you." Rolling over, I pull her into my arms and embrace her. Tears fill my eyes as my love for her consumes me.

"Arity!" Beau cries.

Releasing Gracie, I search for the little boy that squeaky voice came from. It doesn't take him long to pull himself up onto my bed and literally launch himself in my direction.

Opening my arms, I welcome him into Gracie's and my embrace. "Hey there, little man," I laugh while keeping these two tiny bodies secured against me. I will the overload of emotions to settle. A lump takes up residence in my throat.

"Oh my, I'm sorry," Mom laughs when she walks in and notices my now full bed. Gracie and Beau wiggle their little butts under the covers and snuggle in close to me. "Wait there, let me grab my phone for a photo." She exits the room.

"Are we going to have cake today?" Gracie asks, her innocent eyes boring into mine.

"Of course. It wouldn't be a birthday without cake. Maybe you can help me bake one if Mom hasn't already done it." My fingers poke her in her ribs, and she breaks out in a fit of giggles and tries to scramble away. All three of us laugh, and when my focus goes to the door, Mom stands there with her phone in her hand and tears streaming down her face. She gives me a warm smile, which I return before attacking the kids again.

After they're all tickled out, we climb off the bed and make our way downstairs for a "massive feast," as Gracie calls it.

My eyes go wide at the actual feast in front of me. "Wow, Mom, this is too much." My mouth waters as I spot the pancakes and waffles, ice cream, maple syrup, bacon, eggs, and fresh orange juice.

"It's your first birthday with us, and we want this one— and the rest that follow—to be equally as special. We'll do presents as well." She pulls me against her, giving me the tightest embrace.

"Thanks so much. You really didn't need to do this." I choke on my words.

"Yes, I did." She releases me and goes about setting plates out, and we all settle in and have a filling breakfast.

When breakfast is over, I'm so full I think I need to be rolled from the table and out the door to school. I say goodbye to Mom, Paul, and the kids. After I pull the door open, I squeal a little. Jase stands there.

"Damn, you scared the crap out of me. Next time, knock. What are you doing here?" My hand clutches my chest.

Jase chuckles, and it's like it vibrates right through me even though we aren't touching. "Happy birthday. I wanted to give you a lift if that's okay with you."

How could I deny this man? He stands in front of me with a football team shirt hugging his muscles—those same muscles I ran my hands over. And the memory of them are ingrained in my head.

"Oh, hello, Jase. How are you?" Mom comes to stand behind me.

"I'm good, thanks. I'm just picking up the birthday girl."

"Perfect. You better run along now. Don't want you both to be late." Mom hands me my bag that I'd dropped on the floor and pushes me into Jase's chest. Three times the charm. It's becoming regular—these bumps into him. Not that I can complain, though. Raising my hand, I place it on his chest to steady my footing.

"Gee, thanks, Mom. Way to make me feel special," I say, rolling my eyes.

"Don't sass me, girl. I've got things to organize." With that last comment, she shuts the door, and I still haven't removed my hand from Jase's chest. Quickly, I snatch it back and take a better hold on my bag before tossing it over my shoulder.

"Well, I guess we're leaving then."

"I suppose so. Come on." He turns and puts an arm around me, guiding me to his car. Opening the door, I go to climb in and pause. There's a small square box with a tiny red bow resting on top sitting on the passenger seat.

No matter how much I try, I can't hide my smile. "You didn't have to get me something," I gush.

"Who says it's for you? It's Paislee's birthday tomorrow."

My face heats. "Oh, yeah, sorry. Of course you'd want to get her something. Aren't you two good friends?"

Jase suddenly busts out laughing. "I'm sorry, the gift is for you." He comes around and stands behind me, resting his hand on my hip. He leans in and grabs the box. Damn, he smells so good. I turn to face him. We're close—really close. He holds the box out. I take it with trembling hands.

"You didn't have to get me anything."

"Pfft. You deserve something. Not just anything; it had to be special. Open it." He gestures to the box. Smiling, I lift the lid. A gasp escapes my throat. Tears fill my eyes.

"You remembered." My eyes don't move from the charm bracelet in the box. When we were younger, I'd begged my mom for one of these. I'd wanted to save up and buy charms that represented the things closest to me. Lifting the gold chain from the box, I inspect the four little charms hanging on it. There's a football, a phoenix, the letter C, and a piece of cake.

"So, the C is obvious: Charity; the phoenix because they always rise from the ashes; cake because it's your birthday; and the football represents me."

Without thinking, I rise on my tiptoes and wrap my arms around him. He holds me against him. "Thank you so much," I whisper against his neck then place a small kiss there. His entire body shivers.

"You deserve it, and now you can collect the ones you want and that mean something special to you. When this one runs out of room, I'll buy you another."

My chest swells. Jase is a big man on the outside, but on the inside, he's a complete softy. Any girl would be lucky to have him.

Releasing me, he shifts back. "Here, I'll help you put it on." Once he clasps it, it's his turn to lean in and place a kiss on my cheek. "We should go, or we'll be late."

"Okay." The sexual tension ripples through me. My arms want to fly around him, and I want to kiss him senseless. I don't, though.

CHAPTER
Twenty Two

Charity

Yesterday was amazing, and Jase took my breath away with how attentive he was. He made sure my day at school was perfect—well, as perfect as it can be while in classes. Any chance he got, he'd touch me without making it obvious to those around us.

"Are you heading out tonight?" Mom's voice comes from the doorway.

"Yeah, Paislee and I are having a combined party at her boyfriend's place. I hope that's okay?" I rush out the question, panic seizing me.

"It's okay. I'm glad you have a good group of friends looking out for you."

"Me too. What do you think?" I gesture to the black leather leggings and my flowing light-pink top.

Mom steps closer. Her hand cups my cheek. "You look beautiful. We're so lucky to have you here with us, Charity. And that Jase is a sweet guy."

"He is," I agree with a small grin.

"Be careful tonight. I know they're your friends, but as your mother, I worry." She laughs nervously.

"Don't worry, Mom. I'll be with the girls all night. I'll probably stay over at their dorm. So, don't stress. I'll be alright," I say, tugging at my shirt. "I better get going."

"How are you getting there?"

"It's not far from campus, so I'll walk there."

She gives me one of her *I'm not so sure* looks. "It's dark. I don't feel good about letting you walk." When I open my mouth to respond, my phone rings.

"Hello?"

"Hey, is this Charity?" a deep male voice comes through the line. It sounds as though he's driving.

"Yes, it is."

"I'm almost at your address with all of your stuff. Are you home?"

No, no, no. I'm not ready. I don't want to face my demons. The phone drops from my hands.

Mom snatches the phone from the ground. "Hello, who is this?" My ears become muffled to her conversation.

"Charity? Are you okay?" Mom stands in front of me with her face in mine.

I think I nod, but I can't be sure. "I'm going out. I can't deal with this, Mom." My eyes burn with unshed tears.

She nods. "Alright, you go, and I'll deal with everything, and when you're ready, it'll be there for you to go through."

"Thank you," I breathe, even though I feel as though I'm about to have a full-blown panic attack. "I need to go." I don't give her a chance to respond. She hands me my phone, and I'm out the door and running down the street, thankful that I wore the Converse sneakers that Mom and Paul got me for my birthday. They make for an easier escape.

My legs don't stop until I'm standing in front of Parker's place. Music blasts out into the street, and a flood of people walk through the doorway. I need to go inside, but my legs no longer want to push forward. They're planted on the pavement of the sidewalk, so I stay put.

I'm not sure how long I've been in the same spot, but the vibration of my phone pulls me from my trance. It's a message from Paislee, and it's followed by one from Jase, aka Mystery Man.

> **Paislee:** Where are you? Things are getting wild here.

> **Jase:** Are you still going to the party?

I respond to Paislee first.

> **Charity:** I'm out front on the sidewalk.

> **Charity:** Yeah, but maybe I'm not ready to meet you tonight now. Something has happened, and I'm all over the place. Sorry.

Even though I know it's him, I don't think I can bring myself to be happy about it at the moment. A rush of memories featuring my father slap me across the face. It's as if he's standing in front of me and screaming at me, a little spit hitting the corner of my eye as he does. I have to refrain from wiping it away, or he'll full-on spit in my face. A metallic taste in my mouth pulls me back to reality. None of that is going to happen again. My lip is clamped between my teeth, and my jaw is locked.

Moments later, Paislee steps out of the front door and rushes toward me, concern etched in her features. "What's wrong? Come on, let's go enjoy our night." She takes my hand and drags me behind her. My feet move, and my mind buzzes. Paislee has obviously had quite a bit to drink. The minute I step inside the doorway, Addison hands me a drink, which I take.

"Drink that slow or else it'll go straight to your head. Have you eaten?" Addison asks. I find myself nodding. Did I eat? Who cares? Placing the cup to my lips, I tip it back, and the burn that follows is somewhat soothing, but it doesn't erase what's going through my head.

All my stuff is going to be there, and I'm going to have to go through Dad's things as well. All those painful memories stab me in the stomach. A part of me wishes I could set it all on fire.

Loud laughter draws my attention. Turning, I find Jase leaning against a wall with some girl standing super close to him. She laughs again and rests her hand on his arm which is crossed over his chest. My heart aches, and those familiar walls start to rebuild. And my drink suddenly turns sour in my stomach. I should have known this whole thing was too good to be true.

It's like the floor is collapsing underneath me, and I'm Alice tumbling down the dark rabbit hole. Only this one doesn't lead me to all those fantastical places. It's taking me somewhere I don't want to go. A place where broken, damaged, and closed-off Charity dwells.

The voices around me become muffled noise. My eyes roam around the room, and I continue to down the drink

Addison handed me. I have no idea what's in it, but it's slowly numbing the pain coursing through me. I want more.

"You look so pretty tonight, Charity." Paislee pulls me in for a hug. My body has gone into robot mode. I give Paislee a one-armed hug. "Don't worry about her. He's not interested in her," she whispers in my ear before we separate.

"Whatever. I'm going to get another drink. What's in this one?" I hold up my cup to the girls.

My body starts tingling before I even get a chance to walk away. Jase has stepped into our circle. "Hey, ladies. What's going on? Having a good night?" He seems happy.

"Yep, we're good. I'm going to top up." I plaster a fake smile on my face and step away from the group to refill my cup with something strong, or maybe I'll down a few shots to eliminate these stupid feelings.

My eyes roam over the different bottles of spirits lining the kitchen counter. Vodka stands out the most. I pour myself one, and then I toss it back. And then another. When I'm about to throw back the third one, a hand catches my arm. "What the hell do you think you're doing?" Jase's voice sounds furious. His eyes blaze.

Shrugging, I lean against the counter. "Drinking. What does it look like? Plus, I'm enjoying my party. What? Are you going to wreck my night now, being a big macho man again?"

He releases my arm as though I've stung him. "This isn't you." He waves his hands at me and gestures to the drink in my hand.

Rolling my eyes, I say, "What makes you think you know me so well?" My words slur a little, but before he says anything else, I empty my cup in my mouth and grin.

"I know you're not this person. What's brought this on? Has something happened?" He grips my arm in his hand and drags me out of the room and out the back where there are less people. He finds a quiet corner of the yard and releases me. "Tell me what's going on."

I fold my arms over my chest. My eyes hold his gaze. Stubbornness has never been my forte, but the alcohol has given me some strength, which I'm sure will be gone the moment I sober up and reality sets in. "Who cares? I'm enjoying my teen years and doing everything I was told I shouldn't because that stuff makes me a *bad girl*. Did you know I'm a *slut* if I even kiss a boy?" Verbal diarrhea spills from me.

Jase steps closer. I don't stop him. "You're not a bad girl. You're a regular girl experiencing life. You're smart and talented, and you're the girl I've waited for." He's saying all the right things. Everything about Jase is perfect, except me. I'd be that tainted black spot in his life.

"Just don't, okay? I know what I am, and I know I'm not good enough for someone like you. I thought I could be, but not anymore." My body trembles. "Jase, I just don't want to feel anymore. I don't want to hear my father's voice in my head every time I do something. Happiness is what I want, but the minute I get within an inch of it, he's there." Tears slide down my face. It's not going to be a pretty sight since I didn't use waterproof mascara. I couldn't care less, though.

Jase's body is against mine, and he wraps me in his familiar musky scent. A wave of security and calm washes over me. "I can help you if you'll let me. Let me in, Charity. Let me be *your* person."

"I know it's you," I blurt out.

He pulls back slightly but keeps a hold on me. His contact is soothing the turmoil within me. "Me, what?"

"Mystery Man."

"Paislee told you," he says, and I nod. "Good, because I was going to tell you anyway tonight. I'm sick of playing games. You deserve to know it's me."

"I think I should go home. I'm not in a partying mood."

"Did you eat tonight? Do you want to come back to my place until your head settles, and we can get some food into you?"

I shrug. "I can't remember. Everything is kind of a blur. I received a call to say that my dad's stuff was arriving, and it's thrown me. I don't want to deal with any of it." Tears fill my eyes again.

"Come on. Let's get out of here." Jase wraps his arm around my waist, securing me against him, and leads me out of the party.

CHAPTER
Twenty Three

Jase

Of course she'd be thrown with everything that belonged to her father showing up. How is she supposed to deal with all those memories, especially the painful ones?

When we arrive at my place, I help her out of the car. "You could have just taken me home. I feel bad leaving the party the girls put together for me."

"Trust me, they'll think you were there all night. They drink a lot more than you do."

She giggles. "I'm not much of a drinker if you didn't already notice. Perhaps it's a sign that I shouldn't do it."

"That's your decision," I say. "There's no way I'd tell a girl what to do or not to do."

"You're such a gentleman." She playfully pokes me in the chest and laughs. Clearly, those drinks are really hitting her now.

After leading her inside, I sit her down on the couch. "I'll go and put some food together for you. Do you want to watch a movie?"

"I can think of another thing I've never done that we could do."

My body heats with her admission.

Clearing my throat, I say, "Well, maybe not tonight. When you're sober would be a better time for something like that. I'll be back."

There's no way I plan on deflowering this girl when she's drunk. She's everything and more. With her, I have to tread slowly. Baby steps. She's fragile, and who knows what's going to spook her.

I head to the kitchen and get to work. Five minutes later, I return and hand her the plate with a cheese and ham sandwich on it along with a bottle of water. "Here you go." She takes it and places it on her lap before taking a small bite. "You need to eat the whole thing, and I'm sure tomorrow you're not going to be feeling so hot."

"Urgh, I'm not looking forward to that. I can already feel a dull ache sitting in the back of my head. Thanks for looking after me tonight."

Reaching out, I place my hand on her leg and give it a small squeeze. This girl is so much more than what she thinks of herself. "Like I said, I'm here for you. I don't plan on going anywhere. And when you're ready, do you think we could give *us* a shot?"

She starts coughing and choking on her sandwich.

"Here." I hand her the water bottle. She downs a couple of mouthfuls.

"Sorry, my throat is dry. Jase. You're amazing, and you've been so patient with me, but I'm not sure I can do this right now. I'm all messed up." She taps her head, and red-hot anger pours through me.

"You are not crazy. That stupid man who called himself your father wasn't much of one. If anything, you should be doing the opposite of whatever he said. It's all wrong." I sigh and suck in a breath to calm myself down. When I meet her gaze, she's wide-eyed, and I sense I somewhat frightened her. I take her hand. "I'm sorry. It's just when it comes to you, I get so angry when you think you're not good enough. You are—you're so much more than I'll ever deserve. Please believe me when I say that I'd never do anything to intentionally hurt you."

She looks away, and I think I hear my heart break a little. "I know. It's all me, though, Jase. My head and my heart are on two different playing fields at the moment. I want to follow my heart, but then my head gets in my way. It won't always be like this. I need to battle my own demons, and then, hopefully, we can figure things out. You're the right guy in every way. You're perfect. Any girl would be lucky to have you in her life." Her throat catches. Is she telling me goodbye?

"Please, Charity. Don't push me away." My grip tightens on her hand.

Placing the plate on the small table beside the couch, she turns to face me. "I think I should go home." She's become so unreadable. All her emotions seem to have shut down. She's not the Charity who walked in the door with me only moments ago.

"Please," I beg. "Don't shut me out."

She stands and dusts the crumbs from herself. I'm off the couch in seconds. "If you can't take me home, I'll get an Uber." She wrings her hands together. I'm not liking what's happening. How can I stop her? How can I help her?

Sighing, I say, "I'll take you."

The short ride to her place is a silent one. Charity doesn't look my way, and I, in turn, keep my eyes forward, even though there's something pulling me in her direction. When I stop out front, I reach over and touch her arm. "I need you to know something."

"What?" Her voice is almost robotic. She still doesn't glance my way.

"I think I'm falling in love with you, Charity. Please don't shut me out."

She nods and climbs from the car without a word. My heart cracks. Once she's inside, rage takes over, and I smash my palm on the steering wheel. "I'm so stupid." I should have kept my mouth shut. I'm always moving too fast and screwing things up.

CHAPTER
Twenty Four

Charity

As much as I wanted to hear Jase's admission, it's not something I can act on at the moment. Who would ever want a crazy, emotional girl like me? I can't put that burden on him.

I strip off and put on my pajamas. I crawl under the blankets, and even though I'm tired, it's like my body and mind know there's a cloud of uncertainty hanging over me. Knowing all Dad's stuff is packed away near me has me on edge. What am I going to find? Will I find a peace I've been looking for or just more unhappiness? Will I continue to live in fear of what my father has filled my head with?

Jase is the one guy I could easily give my heart to, but it's so hard to release all the fears I have. I don't want to be his burden. He's going places; he has so much potential. And unless I get the help I need, I won't be able to move forward.

Tomorrow I start cleansing, and that means going through and tossing out everything of my father's that causes me pain.

A dip in the bed has my eyes springing open in alarm. "What's going on?" I ask, panicked.

"It's okay, honey. It's just me. I thought you weren't coming home last night?"

After rubbing my eyes, I open them and focus on Mom. "I just felt like coming home," I respond a little defensively.

Mom releases a heavy breath. "Charity, I know it's hard having to deal with this stuff of your father's. I'm happy to help. Just don't start shutting out everyone around you." She gets up and leaves. At the door, she stops. "There's someone here to see you as well."

Before I can ask who, she's gone. Slowly, I drag myself from the comfy spot I just was hoping to lie in all day. Choosing not to change, I head downstairs, and as I get halfway down, my stomach twists in a good way. Jase stands inside at the front door. He glances around until his eyes finally settle on me. Pink hits his cheeks. I suppose wearing my short shorts and singlet top wasn't such a good idea.

"How are you feeling today? I wanted to check and make sure you were alright after last night." Concern in his eyes has me swooning. He really does care.

Descending the rest of the stairs, I come to a stop in front of him. Folding my arms, I say, "I'm okay. Only a small headache." My head stays down because I know the moment I stare into those familiar eyes long enough, I'm screwed.

"That's good. I was hoping we could spend today together?"

"Thanks, but no thanks. Not today."

Jase takes a step closer to me. A shiver runs down my spine. "Charity, please don't shut me out. I care about you."

I move back and glance up at him. "Who could ever want to be with someone as broken as me? On the outside, I appear normal and happy, even. On the inside, I'm a tornado of anger, hate, confusion, and the list goes on. I can't put that on you. I *won't* put that burden on you." Tears sting my eyes.

Jase reaches for me. I twist and move again. "Charity, I know what I want, and it's you."

I hold my hand up, and he stops.

"Just don't. Please leave." Jase opens his mouth—I'm sure to protest—but I simply turn and go back upstairs. My head is already too full and dark. I need to find the light at the end of the tunnel, and I can't do that with Jase around. As much as he says he wants me, I won't be a weight on his shoulders. His own father is burden enough.

After clawing my way back beneath the sheets, I pull the blanket over my head, shutting out the world and drowning myself in darkness.

What feels like hours later, my blankets are ripped from my body.

"What the hell?" I growl.

"Get out of this bed. I won't let you fall into the same pit I did," Mom says. "Now, get out of this bed and get dressed. We're going to put your bed and desk in today."

"What if I don't want to?"

"I won't let you wallow. We are going to work and talk through this. Now go and get dressed, and come have some lunch, and then we'll get started." She exits and takes my blanket and sheet with her—I'm guessing so I can't just curl back up and go to sleep. Gee, she can be a hardass.

Taking my time, I slowly get dressed and then make my way downstairs where Mom has a sandwich with a glass of juice ready for me. She points to a place at the table. "Sit and eat. You're not getting out of this. Paul has taken the kids out for the afternoon."

"I'm not hungry," I grumble.

"I don't care. Take one bite, and we'll get started."

"Gee, drill sergeant much?"

"Don't give me the lip. I've been where you are, only I lost a child. Now she's in front of me, and I can see her spiraling like I did. I won't let that happen to you. You have an appointment on Monday with a psychologist, and we're going to work through your stuff together whether you like it or not. I love you and care about you. And so does that young man that was standing in the doorway this morning." She jabs a finger at the front door. "He told me how you acted last night, and that's the final straw for me. I won't let that evil man break you or break your spirit." Her voice cracks. A weight settles in my stomach as her words slowly sink in.

Reaching out, I take her hand. "Sorry, Mom."

"You're stronger than you think, and you need to give that young man a chance. I'm not sure if you know this or not, but he wrote you letters after you left. He gave them to me to send with my letters and gifts."

"What? I just assumed you both forgot about me. I resented you and hated him. When I first saw him, I didn't want anything to do with him."

Mom shakes her head. "I'm guessing your father destroyed the letters so you would assume that we didn't care about you, and I'm truly sorry he did that. But take my word for it when I say that Jase cares about you, honey. He loves you. He told me so himself this morning." She gives me a weak smile.

"Okay, I'll try to do better."

"Honey, you're already doing better. You don't have to be perfect here. We all love you, flaws and all." She kisses my forehead and walks away with unshed tears in her eyes.

After I finish my sandwich, we head out to the shed. "You ready?" Mom asks as her hand grips the door. "There's a lot of stuff, but we'll get through it."

"Okay." My voice is barely a whisper.

Mom cracks the door and pulls it open. Immediately, I'm slapped with my father's familiar mothball-type scent—one that I'd much rather forget.

"First, we'll get the bed and desk up into your room and then pull the old one apart. Paul will have to help us with the mattress. It is pretty heavy." She laughs a little.

Stepping into the area full of boxes and some small furniture, the urge to run and get some gas and set this place on fire overwhelms me. I hate the man who hurt me, who turned me into this petrified little mouse. But hopefully, with the help from Mom and possibly Jase, I can do this. I am stronger than I believe.

CHAPTER
Twenty Five

Charity

After Mom and I drag what we can up into my room, remove the old bed, and set up my original one, we take a small break. My phone vibrates.

Jase: How are you? I know you told me to leave, but I can't walk away again. I already lost you once, and I'm not going to let it happen again.

"Is that Jase?"

"Yeah, how did you know?" I glance up from my phone. She's taking a bite out of one of her homemade savory muffins.

She smiles. "The way your face changed tells me all I need to."

"How do you mean? I don't think it changed."

"It did. Your smile was instant, and your cheeks went pinker than usual. What did he have to say to cause this reaction?" she teases.

"Nothing much, just telling me that he's not going to leave me alone basically," I say while trying to play it cool, even though I'm buzzing and really just want to talk to him and tell him I'm sorry for how I acted. Mom has really shown me that it's okay to be a little broken and still find love. She won't let me fall, and I have no doubt that Jase would do anything to keep me safe and happy. Now it's up to me. Only, I'm just not ready to let him in until I get my head together. First, I want to get through all of Dad's stuff then erase it from my memory as best as I can.

"He's a good kid, that one." Mom gives me an approving glance before taking our plates and placing them in the sink. "Alright, let's go tackle some of these other boxes before Paul and the kids get home."

Dread pools in my stomach, but it needs to happen.

After opening the first box, I know exactly where it's going. It's full of Dad's clothes. "These are for the trash."

"Are you sure you don't want to donate them? There are people who could wear them." Mom has a point.

"Okay." Closing the box, I slide it to the side where I've already got a pile started for donations. It's got old furniture I no longer want or need and some of Dad's books that were on top of the clothes.

Paul arrives home an hour later, so Mom has to sort out dinner. "Will you be alright? You don't have to keep going without me."

"It's okay. I'd rather get it finished."

"Okay, I'm inside if you need me. Also, I think you need to message Jase back. Your phone hasn't stopped since we came back out here." She grins then heads inside.

Grabbing my phone from the bench, I see there are three messages. One from Paislee and two from Jase.

> **Paislee:** Hey girl, just checking in to see how you're doing? I feel like I've been hit by a car. Never again am I drinking like that. Poor Dane had to carry my drunk ass to bed last night. Good thing he loves me.

> **Jase:** Paislee has called me to find out how you are because she saw us leave last night. I told her you weren't feeling well.

> **Jase:** I really hate not talking to you. Please answer me. Gee, that sounds desperate. Just talk to me, Charity.

Placing my phone down, I get back to work. This job needs to get finished as soon as possible, because I need my father out of my life. I can't erase everything by simply throwing it out, but it can help.

I pull a smaller box toward me and cut the tape with scissors. As I lift the flaps, my mouth drops to the floor. My heart does a flip. Reaching in, I pick up the unopened package. Turning it over, I check the sender. Tears fill my eyes when I see Mom's name written there. There is a heap of unopened packages and letters. My dad had kept them all, but why?

Reaching in, I grab a bunch of envelopes. They're all letters from Mom and Jase. I can't stop the tears sliding down my face. After taking the top one and placing the rest back down, I sit on the concrete floor.

Dear Charity,

I miss you. You are my best friend. Today I started school for another year, and you weren't there. It made me so sad. I sat in class crying. I just want my friend back.

Love,

Jase

A sob rips from my chest. He did miss me. He didn't forget me. Staring at the letter from nine-year-old Jase, my chest feels as though it wants to explode. Emotions I've never experienced pour through me. Jase was my best friend, and he never forgot me. Although, maybe he did as he got older, because even I never expected to come back here. I thought it was always going to be Dad and me. Seems as though fate stepped in and gave me another chance at a happier life. I intend to grab it with two hands and never let the good things be taken for granted.

CHAPTER
Twenty Six

Charity

I'm sobbing on the floor as I read letter after letter from Jase. I come across some from Mom.

> *My darling girl,*
>
> *If you get this, I want you to know that you are my first love. The moment I held you in my arms, I knew you were special. You were my nine pounds of precious, and watching you grow was a blessing. The day your father took you away from me, my heart shattered into a million pieces. I wanted you back so bad. It was as though a limb had been taken from me.*
>
> *Don't believe anything that man tells you. The moment you're able, you come back to me, and I'll keep you safe.*

It's your sweet sixteenth today, and I wish that I could be there to celebrate with you. Every year you'll have received letters and presents from me on your birthday and Christmas, and you'll also find the same from your friend Jase. He misses you; he tells me every day. How I wish I could come and get you, but I can't.

Just remember Momma loves you and always will. I hope we have some time together soon.

Love always, your mom

She and Jase had written me every year. I begin sorting the letters into piles—one for Mom and another for Jase. The two most important people in my life never gave up on me. If anything, they were my silent cheerleaders. I may not have known they were, but reading these letters affirms that they were. I pick one up from Jase that's dated a couple of weeks before my dad died.

Hey Charity,

Well, I'm sure you're all grown up now. I made a promise long ago that I would write, and I've kept that promise. Every year I write and still get nothing back. I'm not sure what's going on, but I'll keep doing this in the hope that one day you'll read these letters, remember who I am, and come home.

We miss you, your mom and I. You were my best friend and I'd like to have you back in my life if possible.

Hope to hear from you soon.

Your friend,

Jase

Without thinking, I scramble for my phone and send a quick message.

Charity: I need you. Come now.

CHAPTER
Twenty Seven

Jase

I bolt upright when I read Charity's message.

    Jase: I'm on my way.

I don't even have to think about it. If she needs me, I'm there. What if something terrible has happened? I couldn't live with myself if I didn't go. She replies seconds later.

    Charity: Come around the back to the shed. I'm in there.

Right away, I know it's got something to do with her father. Thankfully, I don't live far. I'm out the door in seconds and on my way.

After pulling up, I leap from my car and run around the back where she told me she'd be. I stand at the door to the shed, the handle in my hand, hoping she's okay. I twist it and step into a massive mess. Boxes line the walls, and piles of stuff are sorted on the opposite side. How the hell am I supposed to find her in this maze of rubbish. "Charity?" I call.

"I'm over here."

Is she crying? Heading toward her voice, I come up short when I find her on the floor with a heap of envelopes and packages scattered around her. Her eyes are bright red, along with her nose.

I rush to her and wrap my arms around her. "What's wrong?"

"Nothing. Everything is fine. You wrote to me not long ago."

Maneuvering my body, I sit behind her with my legs on either side and wrap her in my arms. "I did." I'd completely forgotten. "You showing up threw me, and I neglected to mention it."

"Look, I found every letter and parcel from you and Mom. You really did never forget me."

Leaning my head against hers, I inhale her apple-scented shampoo. "I never could. But that letter was probably going to be my last. I had to let you go. I hadn't heard from you. I suppose a part of me was hanging on to the hope you'd come back, and then, out of nowhere, you were here."

"I'm sorry for how I've been acting. I didn't want to be a burden on you with my messed-up head and all." She turns her head, her green eyes shining with tears. Without thinking, I press my mouth to hers. My hand grips her neck and holds her against me; I never want to let her go.

"I'll take you, all of you. I love you," I whisper against her freshly kissed lips.

"I love you too. Thank you for not giving up on me."

"I never will."

CHAPTER
Twenty Eight

Charity

One week later

"So, this is officially happening now? You and Jase." Paislee practically bounces in her seat as we wait for the players to run out onto the field.

My grin hasn't been wiped from my face the whole week. "Yep. It's happening."

"Oh yeah, I'm a great matchmaker." She holds her hand up, waiting for a high five, which of course I give her. Earlier this week, I'd filled her in on the letters I found. She was blown away that Jase had actually taken the time to write them to me for so long. He didn't seem like the type, she'd said.

"And how are you with everything about your dad?"

"I'm okay. I went and saw the psychologist on Monday. It was good to offload to someone who can offer the help I need. Jase has been amazingly supportive, as has Mom. So, everything is slowly working its way into place."

"That's really good. I'm happy for you, and I'm so glad you came back into my life."

"Me too," I say.

She opens her mouth to say something but then the crowd goes crazy. Paislee and I stand with the rest of the fans. Clapping and loud whooping come from Paislee and me.

"I think you pair are the loudest here tonight," Elsie says.

Addison and Elsie stand there with handfuls of food and drinks. We grab the food and take our seats.

"Well, we have to be. Charity has to show all the support for her *man*." Paislee gives me a sly grin.

Both Addison and Elsie face me with their eyes wide. "So, you're officially together?" Elsie asks.

"Yep," I respond before taking a sip of my drink.

We watch the game, chatting. Jase keeps glancing up to where we're sitting. He gives me little waves and keeps playing. The simple gesture starts a swarm of butterflies in my stomach.

Our team scores the winning try. The crowd goes crazy. I love the vibe and excitement here. It's electric.

"Where's he going?" Elsie asks. When I follow her line of sight, Jase is heading for the stands. "Oh, I think I know exactly where he's heading."

Paislee shifts to let him in. My eyes follow his every move as he stands right beside me. I stand, and Jase wraps his arm around my waist and pulls me against him then dips his head and his mouth presses against mine. People around us are wolf-whistling and cheering. Heat warms my cheeks.

He pulls back but keeps his head pressed against mine. "I love you. Always have, always will."

Grinning from ear to ear, I say, "I love you too."

His mouth claims mine. Happiness and love is something I'm glad I came home to. Everything I need is here in this town. The man beside me has helped pull me back from hell, and I couldn't be more grateful.

EPILOGUE

Charity

Two years later

"I'm so glad we're doing this and that everyone can make it," I say to Jase while standing in the kitchen of the house we've just purchased. Jase got drafted to the New York Giants like his brother, Lachlan. Lachlan has been a regular visitor to our place, along with my family and his. His dad has backed off a bit now that Jase is in the position he wants him to be in. So long as Jase is happy, then I am as well.

"Yeah, everybody has their crazy schedules now," he says as he gets the steaks ready to grill.

"I know, it's really amazing that all the guys were signed to the same team," I say. Parker, Aiden, and Dane all work pretty amazingly together. Even Aiden got drafted to the NBA. Things were pretty rough between Elsie and Aiden when school ended. He had to go back to Australia until his immigration paperwork was sorted. So, Elsie tagged along and got to meet his family. A month later, they were back, and he went right into training.

Parker and Addison are like the golden couple. They are serious couple goals. Him being the captain has drawn some attention to him and his family. Addison handles it well.

Paislee rings me weekly with updates on what's going on with her and Dane and their lives. She's still head over heels for him.

Jase washes his hands and comes and wraps his arms around my waist. He places his hands on my stomach, rubbing it slightly. "I just can't wait to tell them our news."

"Me either. It's going to be great." Being four months pregnant and keeping it a secret for such a long time has been super hard, but we wanted to wait to share the news until we got all our friends together. I don't think I've left the house unless it's been for a doctor's appointment.

Mom has been on the phone with me almost daily. She's so excited to get baby cuddles and to become a grandma. I'd asked Paul if he would be happy to be called grandad, and I've never seen a man cry like that before, but he did, and then I did, and soon Mom followed. I swear Jase thought he'd picked the wrong family to be a part of in that moment.

There's a knock on the door. Placing a kiss on my cheek and a second rub on my not-yet-showing belly, Jase says, "I'll get it."

I finish cutting things for the salad when I hear the greetings happening at the front door. "Everyone's here," Jase says as he comes back into the kitchen. There's a squeal of greetings. After wiping my hands, I go and give the girls hugs and greet the guys.

We're older but still so close, and our friendship will last a lifetime.

"Perfect! Well, I have wine for everyone." I grab the tray I have set up. "And then we have some news."

"Oh, what is it?" Paislee asks excitedly as she takes a glass from the tray.

"You've finally picked a wedding date?" Addison throws out her guess.

"You're giving up football and traveling the world," Aiden jumps in.

I turn and look at Jase. He takes over. "Good guessing, guys, but there's no date for our wedding yet. But we're happy to announce… we're having a baby," Jase says excitedly. Screams follow.

"Oh my goodness! Congratulations, guys." Parker steps forward and shakes Jase's hand and gives me a small hug. Then follows Dane, who almost gets shoved out of the way by Paislee.

"Baby shopping time," Paislee says, clapping her hands.

"Oh yes, that's going to be fun," Addison says as she gives me a hug. "So, how far along are you?"

"Four months."

"Four months!" Paislee yells. "Why are we only finding out now?"

I laugh. "We wanted to wait until we could all get together and then tell you. Why do you think we've been pushing this get-together for the last two months? I was so sick in the first couple of weeks. It was not pretty. So, when you all start having babies, I can give you all the remedies that helped my morning sickness. I'm an expert now."

"Let's get these steaks on the grill," Jase says as he takes the plate and heads out back. Everyone follows.

Hanging back, I savor this moment. There was a time when I had no one, and now I have an abundance of people in my life who love and support me. My life couldn't be more perfect.

THE
End

Thank you so much for reading The Right Guy. I hope you love Jase and Charity as much as I do.

Turn the page for a look at Lachlan's story, Something Old (The Jilted Series, #1) Grab your copy from books2read.com/u/mlW8oW

And come join my reader group Lovelock's Flock: facebook.com/groups/742675105787263

Chapter One
Scarlett

How did my life end up like this?

For the second time in my short thirty years, I'm sitting in a divorce attorney's office.

"Did you hear me?"

My attention clicks to my soon-to-be, second, ex-husband, Craig. The smug grin on his face makes my hand twitchy. Loving him used to be so easy . . . but it turned into something sour.

"No, I didn't, sorry." I attempt to keep my voice even.

He huffs and rolls his eyes. "That's your problem, Scarlett, and why we're here. You never were present. Your work always took *first* priority. Not me."

My back straightens as I lay my hands flat on the table. I shut my eyes briefly and open them again, staring directly at Craig. "Excuse me! That *work* you speak of gave you the life you've enjoyed living for the past two years, and don't even get me started on your lazy ass."

Vivian lays her perfectly manicured hand on my arm. I snap my mouth shut and bite the inside of my bottom lip. I inhale a large breath through my nose and then release it, hoping to expel the bubbling anger rising in me. My body vibrates. How I put up with this man has me baffled. What the ever-loving hell did I see in him?

Vivian clears her throat and tosses her blonde hair over her shoulder. I hang my head and train my focus on my hands as they rest on the dark-wood conference room table. If I have to talk again, I might not be able to rein in the verbal abuse that threatens to spew from my mouth.

"My client has informed me that she has been the income provider in this marriage." Vivian pauses a moment, and I glance up at her. She winks then continues. "Thankfully, my client listens to her lawyer, and when she was told to get a prenup signed, she did."

I don't miss the smugness emanating from her words. He's paled significantly.

Craig quickly leans into his lawyer and whispers something.

"My client has no recollection of signing a prenup," his lawyer states matter-of-factly.

I shoot a worried glance in Vivian's direction. The soft look of reassurance in her green eyes tells me she has what she needs.

Vivian lifts some paperwork from her file and slides it across the table. "This is a copy that *obviously* has his signature on it. Does he have short-term memory loss? There are even witnesses to the signing, me being one of them." She stops, and a look of confidence passes from her to me. The weight that's been sitting on my chest lifts slightly. Thankfully, I listened to her on this when she shoved paperwork in my face.

I'd thought Craig was different. Most guys who date me don't know that I come from money. Craig, though, is the son of one of my father's business partners.

When we met, he was this sweet, caring guy. We were married within six months. Our families were over the moon, and I was, too—until I noticed the things he'd buy with my money. From there, things went downhill at a fast pace.

He played me.

His lawyer collects and scans the document, and he and Craig speak in quiet whispers.

"Do you think things will go smoothly?" I whisper to Vivian, who's busy shuffling papers around.

She side-eyes me. "Honey, you should have listened to me long ago." Her words sting, but they're true. She warned me. My best friend sighs and faces me. "I've got you. We made sure this prenup could not be bent. Even if he bought things, if he used your money, then it's yours. You own everything, and he has nothing. Anything that's in his name is all he gets, plus whatever he came into the marriage with, which, from memory, wasn't much at all."

I wish I had her confidence. "I'm glad you're on my side," I mutter.

"I always will be."

After a moment, Craig's lawyer clears his throat. "My client wants the apartment in New York."

My attention shifts to him, and I want to vomit. That's my favorite place, and Craig knows it.

"No," Vivian shoots back sternly before I can even protest. Judging by the vein pulsing at her throat, she may not have been expecting this. Neither was I.

"We're not negotiating. He leaves with everything he came into the marriage with. Here's a list of all that my client will be keeping. Your client can have the same apartment he had when they first got married. I believe his father bought it for him." She slides a single sheet of paper across the table to him.

"But . . ." Craig jumps up from his seat. His face is flaming red, and heavy breaths push from his mouth. "I'm *owed* something." It almost sounds like a growl.

His eyes burn into Vivian's.

Her expression is blank and devoid of emotion, very professional. "Craig, you've been married for eighteen months and together for two years in total. All properties are in my client's name, and she owned them before you came into her life. What makes you think you are owed anything? She has worked hard for what she has, but according to my records, you haven't been working for the past six months. You've been living off her hard work since then."

"It's not my fault she's a workaholic and couldn't be bothered with her marriage," he mutters before sitting back down.

"So, me working meant it was okay for you to sleep with someone else? Did she make you feel better? And if you had read the whole document before you signed it, you'd know it states that if you cheat, you get nothing except what you came into the marriage with. Don't give me your sob story, Craig. You made your bed—now you have to sleep in it. Can we finish this up now?" The words rush from me, my chest tight.

Vivian twists in my direction. Her mouth hangs open, and her eyes are wide. "I thought we weren't going to use that against him."

"I was trying to let him keep some dignity. I guess that's out the window now," I whisper.

"How did—" Craig stares at me.

"You may think I had my face buried in my work, but I noticed the little things. I noticed the nights you were gone, the secret calls and text messages. I'm not blind to what goes on around me." I rest back into my seat.

The room turns stale and silent.

Vivian doesn't take too long to bring all the attention back to what needs to happen. Her in a courtroom is powerful; I think men underestimate her. "Well, this should be wrapped up in a neat little bow from here on out. I suggest we just get the paperwork signed and move on with our day." She clicks her pen, rests it on the settlement agreement, and then slides it across the table. The winning grin plastered on her face says it all.

I can't wait for this entire charade to be over. Perhaps I'm destined to become a cat woman. Being alone may not be such a bad thing; it's something I could get accustomed to. My father wasn't around much, Mom kept herself busy, and I seem to marry and divorce any guy that catches my attention. I've learned my lesson now. No more guys—just work.

By the end of the meeting, I walk out with everything still intact—all the belongings I had at the start of our marriage, thanks to Vivian's wise advice. I'd hate to see my publishing business destroyed. It's something that's mine and mine alone.

"Well, that's it, then. Please don't marry anyone else for the time being." Vivian struts beside me, her black, shiny heels clicking on the marbled floor as we exit the building.

I laugh and playfully shove her shoulder. "Thanks for everything."

The lump in my throat thickens; no one wants to admit their husband has been unfaithful.

Vivian's arm wraps around my shoulders. "I'm here for you. Let's grab some lunch and have a cocktail or two. What do you say?"

"No, thanks. I'm just going back to the office and drowning myself in work."

She stops and faces me, the worry lines in her forehead more predominant. Her hands go to her hips. "Don't do that. Don't shut yourself away." *Now comes the lecture.* She crosses her arms over her navy-blue satin top, her cream pencil skirt complimenting it well.

The lasso wrapped around my chest tightens. "I just want to be alone right now. Maybe we can catch up later this week."

Vivian agrees, and we say our goodbyes. I head in the direction of my office a couple of blocks away. It's my safe place. The one thing that keeps me grounded and happy.

I can't believe how my life has turned out. I've messed things up.

The only sound I hear is my high heels clicking on the sidewalk, and I scan all the faces around me. People-watching is something I enjoy. A woman with a baby—perhaps it's a secret baby, and the father doesn't even know the cutie in the pram is alive, but, thanks to fate, when they run into each other at her friend's wedding, love blooms.

Warmth blossoms in my chest. Who doesn't love a good love story? Like the ones in the romance books I publish.

A horn blares behind me. I jump, my heart skipping a couple of beats. I stop and face the road, seeing cars, businessmen, beautiful women.

Across the street, a tall, blond man catches my attention. Squinting, I try to make out his face. It couldn't be. *Is it Lachlan?* No, my mind is playing tricks on me. There are plenty of blond men around. *What would be the odds of me running into my first ex-husband the day I divorced the second?*

My head must be taunting me with past mistakes. That's all I seem to be good at. Bad choices. Poor judgment. Stupid mistakes.

Grab your copy of Something Old (The Jilted series, #1)
books2read.com/u/mlW8oW

To keep up to date with what's happening, sign up for my Newsletter
(app.mailerlite.com/webforms/landing/w4c9g7)

Or join my reader group Lovelock's Flock
www.facebook.com/groups/742675105787263

ALSO BY
Liz Lovelock

Lost Series
The Lost One—Book One
The Missing One—Book Two
Lost Series Boxed Set

Letters in Blood Series
Dear Captor—Book One
With Love—Book Two
Forever Yours—Book Three
Dear Captor Boxed Set

My Guy Series
Monday Night Guy—Book One
My Aussie Guy—Book Two
My Forbidden Guy—Book Three
The Right Guy—Book Four
My Guy Series Complete Boxed Set

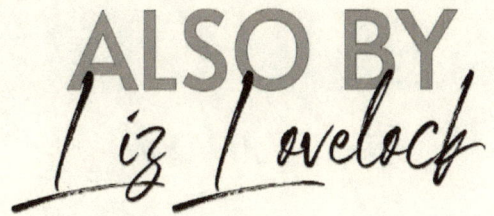

ALSO BY
Liz Lovelock

The Jilted Series
Something Old—Book One
Something New—Book Two
Something Borrowed— Book Three
Something New—Book Four
Something Beautiful – Book Five – A Novella

ABOUT THE
Author

I'm a wife, mother, reader, blogger, and now an author. I'm always busy doing something as I have so much going on, and my three little ones keep me on my toes.

I'm from bright and sunny Queensland, Australia. I have always been a reader. When I was little, I would be up late reading *Garfield* and *Asterix* comic books and also *Footrot Flats*. When I hit high school, they gave us *Tomorrow When the War Began* by John Marsden, and from there my love of books continued to grow.

I keep a notebook and pen beside my bed for when those late-night ideas pop into my head, plus I'm a stationery addict and love pens, notebooks, and, well, anything stationery.

ACKNOWLEDGEMENTS

I'll say sorry first in case I miss anyone.

I'd like to thank my editor—Lauren from Creating Ink and to my proofreader, Jenn from Jenn Lockwood Editing. Without you ladies, I'd be thoroughly lost. You've both pushed me with this one. Thank you for fitting me in on short notice and polishing up my work to make it squeaky clean. You're awesome! Thanks for all your advice and guidance.

A huge thank you to Ben from Tall Story for designing the perfect cover. It is everything I wanted it to be. I love it!

Thanks, Reggie Deanching, for a beautiful photograph of Vince Alexander Azzopardi. You're all amazing.

These next mentions are my other halves in the author world. Without their constant support and friendship, I may have given up a long time ago. They're my cyber sisters spread far and wide around Australia and America, so thank you to Jemma Brown aka JB Heller, KE Osborn, Kaylene Osborn, and Belle Brooks. These ladies are truly amazing. I'd be lost without our chats.

To Anastasia—your help has been incredible. Without you and your input, I'd be all over the place.

To my Flock—I love you, girls. Your support is truly nothing short of amazing. I know I have a safe place in my group with you all. Thank you.

To my readers—I feel blessed to have your continuous support. Thank you.

To my family and my husband—you're truly wonderful. You've never given up on me. You sit and listen when I need to vent out my frustrations, never once complaining about it. I love you.

To my three beautiful children—Millie, Cale, and Finn. You three test my patience, but I'm so grateful to have you in my life to love. Families are forever.

CONNECT WITH
Liz online

Check these links for more information about author Liz Lovelock.

Twitter
twitter.com/LizLovelock

Email
lizlovelockauthor@gmail.com

Website
lizlovelockauthor.com/

Facebook
facebook.com/profile.php?id=100008389321975

Goodreads
goodreads.com/author/show/8268717.Liz_Lovelock

Instagram
instagram.com/lizlovelock/

Or sign up for my **Newsletter**
app.mailerlite.com/webforms/landing/w4c9g7

www.ingramcontent.com/pod-product-compliance
Lightning Source LLC
Chambersburg PA
CBHW020521120726
47904CB00003B/913